SAVED BY A COWBOY

SAVED BY A COWBOY

JULIA DANIELS

TCK PUBLISHING.COM

ISBN: 978-1-63161-061-5

Published by TCK Publishing
www.TCKPublishing.com

Get discounts and special deals on books at
www.TCKPublishing.com/bookdeals

Get special updates directly from the author at
www.juliadanielsbooks.com

C H A P T E R
ONE

"**B**OUT DAMN TIME."

Caleb Kirkpatrick was not a happy man. Shoving his arms into the sleeves of his heavy work coat, he left the warmth of the fireplace to confront his brother Josh. Once outside, Caleb stalked to the van his brother had parked near the main entrance of the Nebraska Sandhills ranch where they lived.

"Where the hell have you been?" Having waited hours for his younger brother's return, Caleb had finally reached his limit of patience and worry. "Cell not working?"

"Well, hello to you, too." Josh laughed and smacked Caleb on the shoulder after jumping free of the rented passenger van.

Caleb followed Josh to the luggage drawers under the vehicle.

"Cell is working just fine. Even called Holly a coupla times," Josh added.

It took a lot of effort for Caleb not to deck Josh for such a smart-ass remark. Josh had called his wife but not Caleb. Josh hadn't even answered Caleb's repeated calls. It was late, and they lived on a desolate cattle ranch, miles from the nearest town. On the winding, hilly, gravel roads leading home, anything could have happened to them.

Caleb looked over to the large, sliding door on the side of the van just as the first passenger climbed out. Josh's brilliant idea. Bring three women out here to the boonies of Nebraska and see which one could out-cook the other two. Reality shows, which forced people to compete for a certain prize, were the current rage on television. Josh thought that if they tried something like that out here in the boonies, it might add some excitement to their tedious lives. A television junkie, Josh watched or DVR'ed every reality show known to man—the goofier, the better.

After sifting through the short pile of online applications, Josh had invited three women, sight unseen. He'd talked with them via telephone, checked their references, and then went and got them, bringing them to the ranch for a month for the competition. Today, Josh had picked them up in a rented party van. He'd covered the whole state, starting in Omaha early that morning.

Would it add some excitement to their lives on the ranch as Josh had suggested? To have three women compete for employment? Caleb was doubtful but willing to give it a shot. He had nothing to lose and a cook to replace.

In the glow of the dome light shining through the open van door, Caleb could clearly see the first contestant. A skinny thing, she looked like the type who'd be more comfortable waiting tables in a sleazy nightclub than cooking stew on a cattle ranch. She wore a tight shirt and even tighter jeans, leaving little to Caleb's imagination. Her heels were several inches high, making her almost as tall as him.

"Welcome to the Morning Glory." He extended a hand, feeling uneasy. What had he let Josh talk him into?

"Hi." She met his gaze, flashing him a toothy smile. Her grip tightened on his hand. "My name's Angel."

"Glad to have you here." Caleb pulled away. "I'm Caleb Kirkpatrick."

He didn't have long to gawk at the sexy blonde. The second woman crashed down the steps. He rushed forward to catch her before she fell into the dust.

"Are you okay?" he asked.

"Yes, thank you." A flush slowly spread across her cheeks.

When she regained her feet and moved aside, he studied her. The overdone, heavy makeup on her face clashed with her demure, modest clothing.

"I'm Phyllis Lamentine," she added, without meeting his eyes.

He repeated the same line he'd given Angel but didn't extend a hand, afraid he might scare her back onto the van.

He felt a little like the single guy on that one matchmaking show, where a limo full of beautiful women drives up to meet him. Except he wasn't looking for a wife, and this was a far cry from a vacation home in Malibu.

When the third cook applicant poked her head out, Caleb stared, slack-jawed. He followed her journey from the van, one step at a time. Why was she here? The lady oozed class from head to toe. The way she carried herself, full of confidence and poise despite being out of her element, impressed him. This was clearly the woman from Chicago. Her dark black hair and startling blue eyes, along with a slightly olive complexion led him to believe she was Greek or Italian. A beauty for sure. How would she fit in here? Worse yet, if he was having this reaction to her, how would his employees act around her? Caleb gave himself a mental shake and looked away.

The women's appearances didn't matter, only their culinary skills. And really, if Caleb had a choice, he'd have his mother do the cooking. The idea of having three strangers in his house, especially three women, was more than a little unsettling.

She walked toward him, the third lady down, holding out her hand, a smile lighting up her face. "I'm Laura."

Why were his palms sweaty? He'd been near plenty of attractive women, so why did he feel anxious in this one's presence? He took her hand and shook it briefly. "Caleb. Your boss." He felt like an idiot the minute those last two words flew out of his mouth, especially when her smile faltered and she pulled her hand from his grasp.

Caleb retreated as quickly as he could to where Josh continued unloading their bags. If he continued talking to Laura, he'd probably say something else stupid.

"So, what do you think?" Josh spoke quietly. "Some nice eye candy."

"That's not why they're here." Caleb shoved his hands into the pockets of his heavy work coat, chilled by the late-September air. "They're here to cook, and that's it."

"Okay. Be that way." Josh winked at Caleb and carried two bags into the house.

Caleb turned back to the women with a sigh. Be pleasant. "Welcome to the Morning Glory. Follow me?"

He turned on his heel and headed inside the main entrance of the lodge. Conner, his young son, stood inside the reception area, wearing his pajamas. With all the commotion, Caleb forgot the boy was waiting to be tucked in.

"Are these the ladies, Dad?" Connor whispered, moving next to Caleb's side.

"Yep, sure are." The look of awe on his son's face made him grin.

Caleb looked back at the women. Did they feel like lambs going to slaughter? They didn't speak, didn't even look at each other.

Angel stared at him, an unmistakable invitation in her eyes. Shy, maybe even embarrassed, Phyllis refused to make any eye contact.

Laura seemed to be studying every inch of the room. Was she impressed? What did the place look like to an outsider? Of the three, she looked the least likely to fit in. With her tailored clothing and high-heeled sandals, she looked as if she belonged on Madison Avenue, not standing in his ranch's dusty kitchen.

"As I said, I'm Caleb Kirkpatrick. This here's my son, Conner."

"I'm six." Conner waved to the women.

"Josh manages the ranch." Caleb nodded toward his brother, who stood on the fringe of the group. "He oversees the men. You ladies will be working under me."

He realized what he'd just said when the blonde smiled and winked at him. "Working for me, that is," he amended.

Angel would give him a run for his money. He could tell that already.

Caleb set down their luggage and rubbed his hands together. Why were they staring at him? "Josh'll show you to your rooms, give you a chance to freshen up. I'll put Conner to bed and meet you back down here in a half hour for some general information."

Just picked up a bag in each hand. "This way, ladies." Josh bobbed his head toward the stairs.

Laura lagged behind and acknowledged his son. "Night, Conner."

Conner waved back and giggled. "She said goodnight to me, Dad."

Caleb watched her leave, feeling like giggling himself. The lady had something special about her.

"What the hell am I doing in Nowhere, Nebraska, population fourteen?"

Laura fell back onto the large bed situated smack-dab in the middle of the spacious, comfortable room she'd been assigned. She kicked off her mules and sank her toes into the plush carpeting, relieved to have a moment of privacy.

You needed to disappear, she reminded herself, closing her eyes and placing an arm over them.

And earlier that morning, at Eppley Airfield, that's exactly what had happened. When she'd found Josh Kirkpatrick holding a sign with her new name on it, she'd realized life as she'd known it was over. Sabrina Marconi had died; Laura Marshall had been born.

The whole thing was crazy. Running from the mob, refusing to enter the protection program after getting shot at by thugs of the Garbaldo family, leaving everything and everyone she knew behind....

Standing with a sigh, she sniffed away the tears that threatened. Wasn't she done crying? She removed her jacket and tossed it across the wingback chair at the window. She dug inside her luggage, found her favorite running hoodie and matching leggings, and slipped them on. Slippers were next, and soon, she felt like she was at home—almost. If she *had* a home.

"Time to start the competition."

She drew one more deep breath, took a quick glance in the mirror, and then she left her suite.

Laura was determined to win. Call it her competitive nature. Call it desperation. She had to stay hidden from the eyes of the underworld. And where better to do it than a place that didn't even register on MapQuest?

At this point in her life, all the money she'd squirreled away since starting her restaurant was irrelevant. Safety was her only concern. As much as it had sickened her to leave her Chicago life; her friends, her family, and her career behind, she had little choice. When the mob orders a hit, the best thing to do is simply vanish. Which is what she had done.

She was a hell of a cook, knew that she could win this job...that she needed to win this job. She had to be almost invisible to avoid the wide, creeping tendrils of the underworld.

She padded down the carpeted stairs and returned to the now empty main room. It was a gathering place of sorts, filled with leather couches and comfortable chairs. She felt like cheering when she saw the note taped to the fireplace inviting her into the kitchen for food.

"So, where is the kitchen?" Should she be worried that she was talking to herself so much? She chuckled and shook her head. Laura walked down the lighted hallway, hoping the kitchen would be at the end.

A veritable smorgasbord lay upon the kitchen counter. She looked at the spacious room briefly but, starving, having avoided food all day because of her nervous stomach, she now focused her attention on the food. Tomorrow would be soon enough to play with the knobs and buttons on the oversized and recently updated stainless-steel appliances. Food was a priority. She greedily filled a paper plate and took a can of diet pop before leaving the kitchen and finding a spot on the dark, fine leather couch in the main room. She dug in, realizing her last meal had been almost nine hours earlier.

"Hungry?" Angel, the sexy-blonde-cook-wannabe, walked in, her hands resting on her thin hips, a sneer marring her face as she scanned the food on Laura's plate.

Laura ignored the woman's jab and continued to eat. She liked food. So what?

"Where's the chow?"

"Kitchen's down the hallway." Laura pointed.

Angel left her, and Laura sighed. That woman would be a difficult one to get along with.

When Angel returned a short time later—with enough on her plate to satisfy a small rabbit—she plopped down onto a wingback chair next to the fireplace. "How long ya think this is going to take?"

Laura rolled her eyes. After picking up Angel, what had so far been a pleasant drive to the ranch had turned into three hours of hell filled with her whining and complaints. Laura had never met someone so impatient in all her life.

"Just long enough." A deep male voice answered from the doorway.

"Oh. Hi." Angel perked up, a flirty smile on her face.

"Hi, yourself." Caleb returned her smile.

Laura grimaced. Why are men so dumb? Angel had flirted with one of the new ranch hands on the van ride here. Now, Caleb was falling prey to her charms. Maybe? Or maybe he was happily married and just enjoying the brief attention from the blonde.

"Your name's Angel, right?" Caleb sat in the chair opposite her, next to the fireplace.

"Yes, it is." She leaned forward, displaying her cleavage. "That's only my name though." Her voice had dropped seductively.

Laura coughed, covering a laugh.

"You're Laura?"

He shifted his attention to her.

"Yes," Laura said.

He folded his hands in his lap and leaned back without any reaction toward her, not even a smile.

She returned his stare, studying her potential employer. What kind of boss would he be? It had been so long since she'd worked for anyone else; Laura hoped she remembered how to follow orders without questioning.

"Am I late?" Phyllis paused right inside the doorway.

"No, just getting started now." Caleb leaned forward, resting his elbows on his thighs. "Welcome, again. I hope you like your rooms. My son and I live in the east part of the downstairs." He pointed out the door they'd come through.

"Josh didn't say nothing about babysitting." Angel frowned.

Caleb opened his mouth and then shut it. He tried again. "My mother takes care of him." A phone rang in the distance. "I have to get that. Phyllis, go ahead into the kitchen and get some food. When I get back, we'll visit."

So, no mom around. Only Grandma. Poor kid.

Caleb sauntered from the room, his Wranglers hugging him in all the right places. His legs were slightly bowed, giving him a distinctive swagger she could only describe as…stimulating.

"Nice place, huh?" Angel asked when they were alone.

"Yes, it is. Bigger than I expected." Laura took a bite of her sandwich.

"All ranches are big in Nebraska. Well, the ones whose owners have money anyway." Angel leaned forward and lowered her voice. "This guy smells like money. He's a fine piece of ass, too."

Laura stared at the girl, wondering what kind of life she'd led before making her way out here. Laura would never admit to thinking what Angel just said, much less saying it out loud to a stranger.

Phyllis joined them with a plate full of food. They sat, waiting in stagnant silence, only broken up with the occasional crackle of wood in the fireplace. Would they turn into friends in the coming weeks—or enemies? Laura hoped the first but believed the second was a more likely outcome.

When she finished her food, she took her plate into the kitchen and nabbed a chocolate brownie. Caleb was back in the main room when she returned, handing out pieces of paper. She glanced at hers briefly, noted it was a contract, and reclaimed her spot on the sofa next to Phyllis.

"I'm going to go ahead and talk while you finish eating. I'm sure you will all want to get to bed, like I do." Caleb leaned against the fireplace and rested his elbow on the mantle.

Laura caught Angel's smirk. Was the blonde picturing herself in bed with Caleb?

Lord, why am I thinking like that? Cooking was all Laura needed to be concerned about. That, and staying hidden from the eyes of the underworld. The last thing she needed was to think of Caleb as anything other than a boss.

But if Angel planned to use seduction to gain an advantage, Laura had to be ready for the fight. She would win the cook-off, no matter what.

She had nowhere else to go.

"Josh gave you all the basics when he invited you three to come out for the month. I decided tonight I would go over the main house rules."

Laura stared at his face as he spoke, distracted anew by his looks. When she'd seen him outside, he'd looked older. Now, in the firelight, the angles of his face were softer. He was older than her twenty-eight, maybe in his mid-thirties, unless he'd faced lots of stress in his life, worries that would have led to the stray grays at his temples and the lines around his eyes. His jawline was strong, squared off; he had a small cleft in his chin, and lips that looked....

"First of all, no men upstairs." The sharp tone in his voice made her focus on his discussion again. "If anything needs to be fixed, you come to me."

"Aren't you a man?" Angel asked in a throaty murmur.

Laura closed her eyes and rubbed her hand over her face, fighting the urge to howl in laughter.

"Yes, ma'am." Caleb nodded. "But I'm also your employer."

Chastised, Angel focused on her candy-apple-red nails.

"Second rule," he said.

Caleb cleared his throat and then shifted his weight from one foot to the other. Was he nervous or had Angel's comment rattled him that much?

"I don't want any direct contact between you and the men. They don't need the distraction."

"What about Josh?" Angel asked.

"He's married, Angel," Caleb answered. "Happily married."

Laura caught the icy gleam in his eyes and was thankful she had not been the one to elicit that response.

"I meant, can we hang out with him?" She rolled her eyes.

"If you have time to do that, then you are not working hard enough." He leaned against the fireplace. "This last thing I ask of you is the most important to me." He placed his hands on his hips and moved away from the fireplace. "Morning Glory is dry. No alcohol or drugs anywhere on the place. I don't employ drunks or stoners."

Minutes passed with no one speaking. When it was obvious he was done talking, Laura lifted the paper resting on her lap.

"Is that all listed in here?" she asked.

"Yep." He nodded. "Plus, it lists the salary for the month. All of you are guaranteed that amount unless you break one of the rules I mentioned. Even if your cooking is awful, I'll pay you for the month."

"No childcare, right?" Angel asked again.

"I answered that earlier."

Tension hung on the air. Laura studied the contract. Phyllis did the same. The rules seemed simple enough. Laura liked wine but could certainly do without her occasional glass. And men? Well, she wasn't here for that. Safety was all she was seeking, in a place she could still continue to bring people pleasure through food.

"Cleaning, laundry, housework?" Phyllis rattled off.

"You'll be expected to do all that, yes."

"Josh never said—" Angel started to argue.

"I'm sure he mentioned housework," Caleb told Angel. "The title of the job you three are competing for is Guesthouse Manager. When we start getting guests after the first of the year, more staff will be added. But for now, you're it."

Josh hadn't mentioned housework to Laura either, but she wasn't about to admit that, not the way Caleb was staring at her. Why was he issuing *her* a challenge? What about Angel? She was the one being difficult.

"Go ahead and read it. The lawyer in town put it together for me." He grabbed pens from the fireplace mantle and handed them out. "Think about it. If you sign it, hand it back in the morning. If not, I'll have Josh run you home tomorrow." He backed out of the room, pausing at the entry. "My mother will see to your breakfast. I'll meet you afterward, seven-thirty or so."

"That early?" Angel griped.

"Early to bed, early to rise. Save anymore questions until then. 'Night, ladies." He saluted them, turned, and walked from the room and into the hallway, back toward the kitchen.

Laura sighed. Let the games begin.

CHAPTER
TWO

DESPITE A SLEEPLESS NIGHT IN an unfamiliar bed, Laura was up at dawn. She dressed, brushed her hair and put it up in a ponytail, and then put in her contacts, ready to grab the day by the horns. Or was that the bull by the horns? Either was appropriate out here on the cattle ranch.

In her old life—in her previous world—she'd spent every evening at the restaurant she owned, paranoid something would happen and too much of a control freak to let anyone else take care of matters. By the time she'd closed up every night, cleaned, and had sent her employees home, it was often midnight. Nonetheless, she was always up early the next morning, ready to do it all over again.

Years spent laboring to build the reputation of Bella Vita had finally begun to pay off. The restaurant was turning a respectable profit. Laura had waitresses she loved, hostesses who schmoozed the customers, which kept them returning. Her food was so good even the oldest matriarch of an Italian family couldn't compete with it.

And now, Bella Vita belonged to someone else.

Laura zipped up her hoodie and grabbed a pair of sneakers from her suitcase. She straightened and then paused. Where the hell was she going to jog? She pulled up the mini blinds on one of the windows and stared and stared at the spacious, empty land she saw in the growing light of dawn. Arriving in the dark the night before, she'd been blind to the beauty.

Corn stood in a field to the south of the house; something short and dark grew to the north. Beyond that, she couldn't see much, other than wide-open sky. She sat down and laced up her shoes, lost in thoughts of this new world. She would miss the variety of the Chicago skyline. Michigan Avenue shops, the lake, the restaurants. *Her* restaurant.

As she left the privacy of her room, the house was silent, but someone was up and about. The smell of freshly brewed coffee greeted her at the bottom of the stairs. Run first, then coffee and a shower.

Curious who the early bird was, Laura walked into the bright-yellow kitchen. Caleb stood at the counter, engrossed in a newspaper.

"Good morning," she said with a grin.

His gaze skimmed her over the coffee mug raised to his lips, his face a blank mask. Would the man ever smile at her?

"Right back at ya."

Laura sighed inwardly. Nothing sexier than a man with a thick morning voice.

He raised his cup in her direction. "Coffee?"

"No, thanks." She glanced at the clock hanging above the professional-grade, stainless steel oven. "So, where are all the cows?" She fingered the zipper on her jacket, suddenly nervous. *What a stupid question, Laura.*

He stared at her so long she felt like squirming.

He finally turned his head the direction of the patio doors and pointed. "About a mile that way." He faced her again. "We harvested that field last week and have them grazing up there."

"I guess I expected them to be closer to the house." She smiled, hoping to get a response, maybe even an elaboration. When none came, she told him, "I'm going for a quick jog. I'll be back by seven thirty easily."

She felt like a cow up for auction as Caleb studied her, his gaze moving from her head to her feet.

"Stick to the road that leads up yonder." He pointed out the glass patio doors to the road Josh took the night before when he'd dropped off the new farmhands at their trailers.

Caleb returned his gaze to the paper laying on the counter, dismissing her.

"Gee, thanks," she mumbled. Should she care he didn't give her the time of day? He was her boss, not her boyfriend. So what if he was hot as hell?

Once outside, she stretched out her muscles, using the porch railing for support. The chilly air revitalized her, its freshness filling her lungs. For the first time in months, she was excited about her workout. She didn't like to exercise, jogged only to work off the high-fat, high-cholesterol diet she couldn't seem to stay away from. Losing some weight had altered her appearance enough so no one from Chicago would quickly recognize her. Not that there was much of a chance of that out here, but running was the only way to work off the bulge that seemed determined to settle itself on her hips and rear.

She took off slowly, passing the glass patio doors, wondering if he was watching her. She picked up her pace gradually as she went and shook off the meeting with Caleb.

Other far more disturbing thoughts danced in her head. Bad memories and a fear she couldn't shake no matter how hard she tried. She'd hoped once she arrived out here it would be easier to let go of her old life, to move on.

Jogging up a small rise, she kicked her pace into a higher gear. The gravel was more of a challenge than she was used to, making her work harder. She glanced at her watch and calculated how long she had before turning back.

Her mind wandered again, the pain of loss still so fresh. Not only had she been forced to say goodbye to her family, she'd been forced to say goodbye to her whole life. Pop had made the mistakes—not her, not her siblings. But Pop was dead, killed by gangsters who wanted to hand her the same fate.

If they found her.

That was why she was now in a hiding on a cattle ranch, farther from a Macy's Department Store than she'd ever been in her life.

Panic swirled through her head, and just as her psychologist had advised her to do, she talked herself through it. "He can't get me. He's not going to find me. I'm safe." She repeated those words like a mantra, louder and louder, over and over again, matching her words with her steps, until her fear receded. How would Ernesto and his henchmen find her when *she* barely knew where she was?

Tears streamed from her eyes, but crying made her run even harder, pushing her muscles to ease the sadness and anger in her heart. Hell would have been much better than the drama she'd been through the last few months. Pop's murder, running from the dangerous mob boss, leaving her wonderful restaurant behind. Losing her family.

She had nothing left.

Not even her real stinkin' name.

"Get a grip, man."

Caleb downed the remainder of coffee with one large gulp. He glanced at the road Laura was following and shook his head, frustrated by his reaction to her. He hadn't felt like this in years, not since Christie left, and he had learned his lesson. He would never let himself get close to another woman. Except for his son, nothing good had ever come from giving his heart to a woman.

He couldn't deny that Laura had inched herself under his skin already. Standing next to her in the kitchen had been pure torture. His physical reaction was so strong, and his treacherous body reacted in a purely male, totally uncomfortable way. He'd had to look away from her, try to focus on a day-old newspaper or he might have burst at the seams. Was it just the length of time he'd been without a woman that brought on these intense reactions, or was it the woman herself?

The night before, when she had stepped out of the van and smiled at him, the chemistry was immediate. Now she had the nerve to be up before dawn, ready to start her day. If her cooking was even edible, she would win the damn contest.

But then again…. Did he want someone he was attracted to working here? He respected women, but he didn't have a spot for one in his personal life again. He needed someone to cook and clean. His heart could not take anything more, even if his body seemed unwilling to agree.

He filled his large, stainless steel travel mug and washed out the glass coffee carafe. Hearing Ma's car coming up the drive, he refilled the coffeemaker so she would get a fresh pot.

He sighed, anticipating his vivacious mother's entrance.

"Hey, doll." She walked into the kitchen and settled her belongings on a chair at the kitchen table. She hung up her coat and pushed up the sleeves on her World's Greatest Grandma sweatshirt.

"Hi, yourself."

"Josh get back last night?" she asked, taking an empty mug he offered her.

"Finally, yes." He watched her carefully take the glass carafe from under the pot that was still filling up. The hot metal plate sizzled as the drops of fresh coffee hit it.

"What are the girls like?"

"Hard to tell. They're all really different." Caleb leaned against the counter. "Haven't met the two new ranch hands yet, either."

"I'm sure the men look like the other yahoos you got out here. What I was curious 'bout was that gal from Chicago. Still wondering why in the world she would come all the way out here."

"Adventure?" Caleb shrugged, wondering the same thing. "She's a class act, too. I doubt she'll make it here a whole month. She's a city girl."

"Now, don't go thinkin' that way." Ma pulled out some pans from under the counter and set them on the stove. "Only matters if she can cook. Fancy manners don't count out here, don't make much difference."

Caleb shrugged. She had a point.

"I'll bet she's hidin' from someone." Ma flipped on a country radio station and moved to the refrigerator to start pulling out food.

"Josh did background checks for all of 'em. Laura is clean. Perfect references." He wanted to add what Josh found out about their stepfather but kept that little piece of information to himself. For now.

"I don't mean that kinda hiding." Her hands balled up on her ample waste. "More like from a man."

"Well, that's none of my business." But Caleb knew he was kidding himself. "Sure you don't just want to stay on?" She was quick and efficient in the kitchen. "Leave that Hank once and for all?"

"He ain't so bad most days."

She wouldn't meet his eyes, and Caleb knew she was lying.

"He's puttering around out in the building a lot or in town," she said.

"You know you got a place out here if you change your mind."

Caleb watched her crack the eggs and whisk them like a pro.

"You get to work, boy. Don't be worrying about your ma. I'll be just fine." She paused to pinch his cheek as if he was still a small child.

"I told the girls I would meet them here at seven-thirty, but it was just a test to see if they are punctual. Suppose you remember when they show up and let me know?" He kissed her cheek. "I got to go meet the new men, get them out to the field to harvest the west eighty acres. They're calling for rain tomorrow."

He whistled as he left the kitchen in his mother's capable hands. What would day one of the Cook-Off Challenge bring?

Laura stopped jogging as she neared the house, slowing to a fast walk. A white pickup was pulling out of the garage just as she neared it. She waved to Caleb, pleased he nodded a greeting. Where was he off to? A Cadillac the size of a boat was parked right in front of the entry.

She moved to the entrance of the home and stopped just inside the door, hearing a woman's voice belting out a twangy, off-key country song.

Even though she was certain she looked like hell, sweaty and flushed from her exertion, she needed her first cup o' Joe. Caleb was gone, and she really didn't give a fig what her competition thought about her looks, so she stepped inside the bright kitchen.

A broad-shouldered, wide-hipped woman with hot pads on her hands was leaning into the spotless oven, pulling a pan clear of the heat.

Laura waited until the oven door was shut before announcing her presence. "Need some help?"

Quick as a tornado, the woman whipped around. "You scared me, girl!" Her empty hand rushed to her chest, a look of shock across her face.

"I'm sorry!" Laura rushed forward. "Are you okay?"

"My stars, yes!" the woman breathed. "I wasn't expecting anyone yet." She glanced up at the clock. "Caleb said seven-thirty."

"Oh, right." Laura leaned her hip against the counter. "I just got back from a jog and heard music and smelled food and, well…." She shrugged and smiled. "I'm Laura." She held out her hand, still struggling to remember her new name and get into the act of her new life.

"You're Laura, huh? The gal from Chicago? Well, hi there. I'm Mary Grace. Caleb and Josh's ma." She shed the hot pads and shook Laura's hand before stepping back to look her over. "You'll do just fine. I can tell already, just by the look of you."

"Really?" Laura laughed. "All sweaty from my run?"

"Well, now." Mary Grace rubbed her hands together. "It's hard work out here, but that's not what I mean." She studied Laura. "You're not rail-thin, so you like to eat and probably like to cook what you like to eat, right?"

Laura nodded.

"Your hands, too." Mary Grace grabbed them, turned them over. "Well-groomed but no polish or rings to get in the way." She laughed. "I love to be in the kitchen, do fine for myself and Hank, but when the boys asked us to move up here and for me to cook for the hands, I said no way."

"Too much work?" Laura snatched a piece of sliced cheese off the tray on the counter.

"At my age? Yes." She nodded, agreeing with herself. "Your age?" She pointed at Laura. "No." She rested her hands on her ample hips and tilted her head. "How old are you?"

"I thought women weren't supposed to say?" Laura chuckled. "I've been legal for quite some time, Mary Grace." She found a mug and filled it with coffee.

"Well, you'll do just fine." Mary Grace repeated her initial reaction. She placed the ham-and-egg casserole onto a different dish. "Caleb is a cranky man, hard to get along with sometimes." She shrugged and paused. "I think it's 'cause he lacks a good woman."

"How's that?" Laura sputtered on her sip of coffee.

"Josh has a woman in his bed every night. Pretty girl, too. Holly. And you'll like her. Caleb, well, if I were a gambling fool…." Mary Grace lowered her voice and took a deep breath. "Let's just say it's been a while since he's had someone special in his life."

Laura could relate to Caleb's plight, but her cheeks still grew warm with embarrassment. She was amazed by the direction of the conversation and darted her gaze to the clock, wanting to look anywhere but at Mary Grace. She cleared her throat. "On that note, I've got to get showered and back down here. Unless you could use some help?"

"No, you go on ahead. You'll have more than enough to do in the next few days." Mary Grace paused while serving the food. "Glad to know you, by the way. Hope I didn't embarrass you?"

"Oh, no. You made me laugh. Something I haven't done in a very long time. Thank you for that." Laura started to leave the room when the older woman asked her to wait.

"Caleb won't be here when he said. Just wanted to test you ladies, so take your time getting cleaned up. Don't tell the other two, though."

Laura went up the stairs, shaking her head at having met a woman who obviously felt no discomfort over sharing her son's private life with a stranger, wearing her hair in a high beehive do, and driving a vintage caddy. One competitor, Phyllis, had admitted to Laura she used to be a nun, and the other was someone who obviously needed a ton of prayers, and then there was Laura herself, who was not at all what she was being forced to pretend to be. Could Caleb have chosen a weirder group?

C H A P T E R
THREE

"**Y**ou're late," Phyllis told Caleb as he entered the kitchen. It was an hour past the appointed meeting time. Laura hadn't minded the wait. She'd eaten breakfast and watched the morning news, easing into the day. Caleb's delinquency had bothered Phyllis, who commented more than once on how she valued schedules.

"Glad you ladies are more punctual than I am." Caleb filled his coffee mug and joined the three cook competitors and his mother at the table.

Interesting response. He didn't apologize or come up with a lie to cover his tardiness. Could she trust him, or would there be mini-tests like this all along the way?

"There's some food left on the stove if you're still hungry, Caleb." Mary Grace glanced up from her crossword puzzle.

"No, thanks." He took a sip of coffee. "Let's get started?"

"Sure." Angel drummed her fingernails on the table. "We've been waiting here awhile."

Some longer than others, Laura added silently. Phyllis had been there when Laura arrived. Angel had just barely beaten Caleb to the table.

"Fine, then." He nodded. "Let's start with the schedule. I've got the next three days figured out." He shifted on his chair and pulled out a sheet of paper from the back pocket of his jeans. He handed it to Phyllis. "After you look at it, I'll post it on the wall over there." Caleb pointed to the cork bulletin board next to the patio doors. "You'll each do a meal a day and a share of the household chores. Weekends, we operate differently. That's why I did only today, tomorrow, and Friday."

"Who's got lunch today?" Angel asked.

"Laura," Caleb answered, drawing her attention back into the conversation. "Phyllis has dinner. Person with the next meal cleans up the previous. So, Phyllis, you'll come in after lunch and take care of the dishes and clean up the kitchen. Laura, you get the honors now."

"Is there a menu to follow?" Laura stopped wiping her mouth when she realized Caleb was scrutinizing her movements. She stared back at him, wondering what he was thinking. *No complications, just let me cook,* her mind shouted.

"No. In fact," he said, stretching his arms in the air and then folding his hands behind his head. "That will be your first challenge. Until I post a new schedule, you'll have to use whatever supplies we have on hand. I call the groceries into the store in town once a week, and they deliver."

"Why doesn't your mom just bring stuff up to the ranch?" Angel looked at Mary Grace.

"She's not an employee of the Morning Glory." Caleb leaned back on his chair and crossed his arms. "It's more efficient to have the goods delivered."

"Do you take inventory when it comes, or will we?" Laura asked.

She didn't quite understand the look he gave her. It was an innocent question.

"I always have. Stella, the woman one of you will replace, didn't read English, and—

"How could she not read English?" Angel laughed.

Caleb's sexy jaw muscles clenched.

"It was just easier, I'm sure," Laura interjected. "When it came to paying the bills, you knew what was coming in."

Her comment quieted the table, and she caught a grateful look from Mary Grace.

"Has Stella left the area?" Laura asked.

Caleb met her eyes. "Her husband worked as a ranch hand here for almost ten years. She's cooked here for about as long, at least since her youngest started school." Caleb studied his coffee mug. "Last month, Juan got sick. They're at the Mayo Clinic in Minnesota just now, having tests run."

Caleb put up a hard exterior, like Mary Grace suggested, but Laura could sense some cracks in his armor.

"What about your kid's mom?" Angel stuffed a muffin into her mouth.

Mary Grace clucked her tongue. "That's none of your business, dear." She stood and began to clear the table.

"Morning." Little Conner, still rubbing sleep from his eyes, came through the kitchen door and stopped next to Laura's chair. "This is my seat."

"Oh…" Laura chuckled.

"Conner—" Caleb and Mary Grace scolded simultaneously.

"Here you go." Laura stood and held the chair for him. She picked up her empty plate. "You want some of Grandma's yummy muffins?"

"Yeah."

Laura put her dirty dishes into the sink. She piled several small muffins on a fresh plate and gave them to the little boy.

"Conner, next time you will ask politely for someone to move. And make sure you thank Miss Laura. You hear me?" Caleb instructed his son.

"Thank you, Miss Laura."

"You're welcome." She felt weird standing in the middle of the kitchen, so she moved behind the granite counter.

"Well." Angel shoved her empty plate to the middle of the table. "Since I have the day off, I guess I'll go on up to my room and unpack." She smirked in Laura's direction before heading for the door.

"Angel, hold up." Caleb waited until she turned around. "Today is your laundry day."

"Ahh." The muscles in Caleb's back relaxed, one by one, as he sprawled across the oversized leather couch in his private living room. He pulled Connor next to him and clicked the television remote to the little boy's favorite cartoon channel. This was the best time of each day, just before bed, when he could shut off the responsibility of the rest of the world and just be a dad.

He leaned his head back and closed his eyes. Day one of his current challenge had been interesting.

Phyllis was quiet and reserved. There were times she was around when he didn't even notice her. But if that night's dinner was any indication, she could cook. Angel, the little temptress, spoke off the top of her head, her immaturity obvious and annoying. When it came down to the final choice, he'd have to think about his future, paying guests. Her current attitude wouldn't work here. She could change, though. Plenty of farmhands started out green and ended up becoming fine workers. Juan was an example.

Angel had a long way to go. She had done the laundry, her only assigned chore for the whole day. Instead of finishing it, folding the clothes, and putting them away, she had left them all sitting in wash baskets and in piles on the counter in the laundry room.

What would it be like if she had all three meals to prepare and housework chores too? Would the house be in chaos? He'd find out in a week, when the women were given a whole day to manage.

He had to shape Angel up quickly or the next month would be very long. He'd talk with her while she made breakfast. He hoped she'd be more punctual tomorrow. The men didn't like to wait on food.

Conner laughed, and Caleb opened his eyes to see a yellow sponge creature named Bob jump off a pineapple on the TV screen. He kissed his son's head and closed his eyes again, trying to relax.

"Dad? Mickey's mom is making him a costume for Halloween. Think Grandma might make me one, too?"

"I'll bet she would." Caleb opened his eyes. "What do you want to dress up like?"

"SpongeBob!"

"I should have guessed." Caleb laughed. How would Ma make a sponge? "We'll ask her tomorrow, okay?"

Conner nodded and settled back into the cartoon until another commercial came on. "Dad?"

"Hmm?"

"Would you tell me about my mom again?"

The million-dollar questions. They came once in a while. Tonight, they were likely a result of the new women in the house.

"What do you want to know?" Caleb asked quietly.

"Where is she?"

Caleb sighed and held him tighter. "Well, like I told you, she likes to ride horses in the rodeo. So, I guess that's what she's doing now." He hadn't heard from her in years.

"She loved horses more than me?"

That one always hurt the most. And the lie he followed it up with was just as painful. "No, she just didn't want to live here with me, Connor. She loved you lots."

That seemed to satisfy the boy for the moment, as it always did. These were the hard questions, the ones he'd rehearsed answers to in the quiet hours of dawn when he wondered the same things. What was Christie doing now?

"I miss Stella and Juan," Connor said on a yawn.

"I do, too," Caleb agreed.

"Think one of them new ladies might like me enough to stay? Maybe be a new mom for me?" Connor snuggled up closer to Caleb's side. "You don't got a wife," he continued. "None of them got husbands. Think you might love one?"

Aw, hell. Where did that come from? "They're here to take care of the house, Con. Not to marry me." No sense getting the boy's hopes up.

"The yellow-haired lady is real pretty. I like Miss Laura best, though, 'cause she talks to me."

Like father, like son. Laura was the woman giving Caleb fits too. Beautiful and refined, smart and articulate, he didn't know how to act around her. He felt slightly intimidated by her.

She could cook too. He'd never been a great fan of fish, but the salmon sandwiches at noon—she called them panini or some such thing—had been delicious. His mother had been the last to order supplies and as she was forever complaining he didn't eat enough fish and needed omega three, whatever that was, she'd stocked up on every sort of fish. If fish would always taste as good as the meal they'd had at noon, maybe he'd become a convert.

Was Laura dominating his thoughts because she was a puzzle? Why had she come here from Chicago? He was paying well for her services, but what did a city girl know about ranches? Phyllis and Angel lived in Nebraska, knew what life out here would be like. Could Laura adjust?

Maybe he needed to go for a jog with her. Find out why she was really here. He chuckled then, imagining himself trying to run.

"What's funny, Dad?"

"Nothin'." He laughed again.

He was crazy, feeling things for her he didn't want to feel. Desire and lust he didn't welcome and knew he had to avoid.

"Time for bed." The credits were rolling already, and Caleb didn't like the direction his thoughts were headed. He didn't want to field any more questions, either. Caleb clicked off the TV and herded Conner to bed.

Caleb's room was on one side of the sitting room; Connor's was on the other side. The whole house had been remodeled during the past two years. With a little extra financing, he had decided to take the plunge and had switched the Morning Glory from his family ranch to a guest ranch to bring in extra income.

Caleb tucked Connor into bed, kissed him on the forehead, and gave him his teddy bear. "Night, Con."

"I really like that Laura girl, Dad. Think she'll be the winner?"

"We'll see, Connor. We'll see." Caleb had been thinking of little else since the woman got here.

Caleb left Connor and walked across to his own bedroom. Was it just hormones? Friday, he'd find out. A band played at the bar in town, and he'd text one of the girls he sometimes hooked up with. Maybe, just maybe, he'd give in this time, and take a little of what Jenny was only too happy to offer.

Anything to get the beauty from Chicago off his mind.

"What the—?"

Laura looked up from the stove and smiled at Caleb. Oh, yum. That hunky cleft in his chin made her smile grow even wider. His short brown hair was slicked back, still wet from the shower. His standard-issue jeans molded to him better than Levi intended, hugging his butt like a glove. She snapped her head up, away from the huge buckle on his belt that rested above a part of his anatomy she needed to ignore. Embarrassed, she focused her eyes on the words Morning Glory, written in red letters on his denim work shirt.

"Morning, boss." She flipped her gaze to the stove, breathing deeply, trying to rein in her attraction. He was just a guy. Beautiful, but just a guy.

"What are you doing?"

She looked back at him, catching an expression of reproach crinkling the corner of his eyes.

"Um…frying bacon?" She grinned. "There'll be eggs and biscuits, too. If they turn out." She turned away from him, her attention on the bacon, which was ready to be turned.

Out of the corner of her eye, she saw him walk to the duty roster posted at the door, and immediately, she understood his confusion. She met his gaze with raised, freshly plucked eyebrows, ready for the confrontation.

"You are not Angel."

"Thankfully, no, I am not." She leaned over and propped open the oven to check the biscuits.

"Where is she?" His voice grew gruff.

"Sleeping." Without elaborating, she pulled the second sheet of buttermilk biscuits from the oven. "Would you care for one?" With hot-pad-encased hands, she held the baking sheet out to him.

"No." He shook his head and then changed his mind and grabbed one. "Yes." He opened the biscuit in half and glanced around the kitchen. "Do you have the—?"

"Over there, on the table." She pointed with the tray.

"—honey." He finished his thought and meandered to the condiments.

"Coffee is ready." She watched from under her lashes as he slathered honey on his biscuit, and then she turned off the bacon. She already missed her cookware. Strange, how a person gets attached to silly things. She drained the grease into an empty can and put the bacon in the oven to keep it warm.

Caleb poured himself a cup of coffee and then leaned his hip against the center island to watch her work. It was mildly disconcerting, really. She knew how to run a kitchen, was confident in her cooking abilities—all of Chicago was confident in her ability to create amazing dishes. His maleness, on the other hand, was troublesome and more than a tad distracting.

"This is quite possibly the best biscuit I've ever eaten." He plucked another from the cooling rack. "Now, Miss Marshall, kindly tell me why you're in the kitchen, creating culinary delights, while Angel is upstairs sawing logs."

He inhaled the second biscuit.

She whisked the eggs, added milk for fluff, and threw them in with the peppers and onions that were already simmering in the pan.

"She was throwing up."

He reached for a third biscuit, and Laura slapped his hand away. "Stop that or we won't have enough." Then, when she realized what she just done, her eyes widened. "I'm sorry; I shouldn't have done that."

He smiled at her. Finally.

"No problem." He devoured the third biscuit he'd pilfered anyway, and then wiped his fingers on her dishtowel. "Listen, Laura. Don't get me wrong. I appreciate you filling in, but if one of you gets sick, I should be the first to know."

"Point taken." She'd been an employer, would have expected the same. But really, Angel had been in no shape to track down Caleb.

Breakfast was the meal she had the least experience preparing, especially a meal to accommodate so many. But, courtesy of Nonna Vita's biscuit recipe, she had produced a winner.

She placed the finished eggs into two large bowls just as the door to the dining-hall area opened, bringing in a whoosh of cool air. Laura reached into the oven, took out the bacon, and laid it on a warming tray. She shoved the bowls of eggs into Caleb's hands and shooed him out of her way.

She set the bacon and biscuits on the buffet-style table in the hall and returned to the kitchen for the gravy dish and condiment tray. Caleb followed her back to the kitchen once all the food was sent out.

"Should I check on Angel, ya think?" He shoved his hands into his pockets.

"You're the boss." She raised her eyebrows and turned her attention to the pans soaking in the sink.

"That's Phyllis's job." He gestured lamely at her cleaning.

"I run my kitchen the best way I see fit, Caleb. That's part of the creative freedom clause you threw in the contract. I clean up after myself." Laura opened the dishwasher and blew out a deep breath. It hadn't been run after dinner the night before, was crammed full, and smelled rank.

"Sorry." He walked up next to her, his thigh brushing against hers. "My fault."

"How's that?" She turned slightly, intimidated by his height.

"Angel didn't clean up after dinner," he said. "I did."

"Oh." Laura nodded but didn't move. How could she when he was looking at her like *that*. She swallowed the lump in her throat and wiped her sweaty hands on her jeans. "No problem," she finally said. "I'll just run it now."

She pulled pans from the dishwasher and added them to the soapy water in the sink. When she turned, Caleb was still there with a heat in his eyes she recognized as lust but couldn't quite believe. Caleb's eyes darkened, and if she didn't know better, she would have thought....

"Good morning!" A cheerful Phyllis bounded into the kitchen, breaking the tightly woven spell Caleb had created.

Laura turned to the sink and scrubbed the pans to cover her discomfort.

"Hello, Phyllis," Caleb said. "I'll go join the men for breakfast."

Back to business, it seemed.

Laura glanced over her shoulder and watched him pull a notepad from one of the kitchen drawers and a pen from his chest pocket. He scribbled down a number and handed Laura the paper.

"Here's the cell number. If I'm in one of the deeper valleys, you may not get me, but if you ladies need me, don't hesitate to call." He looked at Phyllis. "Ma will be up to fetch Con for school."

"Have a nice day." Phyllis waved.

After he left, shutting the door to the dining room behind him, Phyllis turned on Laura. "So what'd I interrupt?"

C H A P T E R

FOUR

"**H**MM?" Laura deliberately kept her voice low. In the adjoining dining room, the men were loud, involved in their own discussions, but the kitchen echoed, making every sound audible elsewhere.

"Oh, please! I'm not blind. There was something spicy happening in here." Phyllis walked up to the center island and rested her hands on the countertop.

"Amazing." Laura laughed. "You do talk! I didn't think you'd ever have a conversation with me." She wasn't ready to even consider what almost happened with Caleb—at least, what she *thought* almost happened—much less discuss it with a stranger.

"I'm quiet most of the time. Comes from my old life." Phyllis shrugged.

Laura wondered if she would elaborate.

"I'm just checking out the situation before I jump in." Phyllis pulled out one of the stools and took a bite of a biscuit. "This is heaven, Laura. Who taught you how to make this?"

"Nonna Vita. My grandma." Laura filled the dishwasher with soap crystals.

"Mine, too!" Phyllis slid off the stool and shut the door that separated the kitchen from the men's dining room, muffling the noise. "Won't you let me help you clean up? I know you told me yesterday you wanted to do it yourself, but, well—"

"No problem." Laura shook her head. "I feel better when I tie up all the loose ends myself."

"So, do you think he's divorced?" Phyllis sat back on the stool.

"Caleb?" Laura walked to the work schedule to double check her next chore. She turned to face Phyllis. "Wonder if we should call him Mr. Kirkpatrick?"

"No idea." Phyllis shrugged. "I mean, with the boy and all, there had to have been a woman at some point, right?"

"I guess." Laura chuckled. Phyllis zipped between topics so fast, Laura felt like a participant in a ping-pong tournament. "It takes two to tango."

"He's handsome, don't you think?" Phyllis whispered.

Laura rolled her eyes.

"Well…. *He is.* Not that he'd ever have anything to do with *me.* Heck, with Angel around, I doubt *any* of these men would have anything to do with me." Phyllis pouted.

"Don't sell yourself short," Laura said, and then, reminded of Angel, thought to inquire about her. "Is she still throwing up?"

"Yeah. I told her she'd have to clean it up herself. I was on the schedule for cleaning bathrooms today." Phyllis swiped the biscuit crumbs from her hand. "No way I'm cleaning *that* up."

Laura flipped on the small television hanging under the counter, glad to have news in the background as she finished washing the pans she'd just let soak in the sink. "What are you making for lunch?" she asked over her shoulder.

The two women chatted while Laura finished cleaning up. Once she got going, Phyllis could talk up a storm, and Laura was glad for the company. Before going out to work, a couple of the men came into the kitchen and thanked her for breakfast, especially the biscuits. Maybe she had scored some bonus points today?

"Hello, hello!" Mary Grace called out.

The front door slammed with a resounding thud, and then the older woman stepped into the kitchen. Laura had just put the last pan away and was hanging her apron over a kitchen chair to dry.

"Hi," Laura said.

"Missing one girl, huh?" Mary Grace grabbed the last biscuit. "May I?"

"Go ahead," Laura said. "Less for me to throw out."

"Could you get some cereal out for Connor? Oatmeal maybe?" Mary Grace asked her, as she headed out the door. "He's always starving when he gets up."

"Well, I don't know how you're feeling," Phyllis said once Mary Grace disappeared through the doorway. "But Caleb's liking what he sees when he looks at you."

"Right," Laura scoffed.

Laura pulled out a packet of cinnamon apple instant oatmeal and dumped it into a glass bowl. She added the necessary water and set it in the microwave. "I'm not here looking for a man."

"I am," Phyllis admitted with a wink.

"Really?" She never thought to question the motives of her two competitors. The job seemed pretty straightforward. A cook position in the middle of God's country that paid better than a four-star restaurant in Chicago.

"Think about it," Phyllis continued. "A lot of men, stuck in the middle of nowhere, no women, no entertainment." She shrugged. "I guess it was kind of romantic to think I could find someone, but I'm almost thirty-five and don't exactly have men banging down my door."

Laura studied Phyllis. She looked younger than thirty-five.

Saved from a response by the beep of the microwave, Laura finished up Connor's oatmeal, added a pinch of sugar, and stirring it into a cartoon character cereal bowl. She filled a matching cup with milk and set it on the table.

"Anyway," Phyllis continued, "I didn't mean to embarrass you. It just seemed like a good spot to meet a man. I do like to cook, but I had other motives."

"Glad you shared that, but I'm just here to cook." Laura smiled. "And clean, it seems, and do laundry." She laughed.

Laura left Phyllis in the kitchen and walked into the dining area to pick up the dirty plates. She expected tons of leftover food, but the serving platters were almost empty. She smiled. How flattering! What would they think about her ravioli for dinner?

She scraped all the food scraps onto one plate. This would be the part of the job she would hate. Busing tables when she was a teenager had pissed her off, but at least then she'd gotten a portion of tips at night's end. Here, she would just get broken fingernails. She straightened the tables and chairs and turned off the big-screen TV.

Back in the kitchen, she set the dishes in the sink and watched Mary Grace tie Connor's shoes. "Did you sleep well, Conner?" Laura asked.

"Uh-huh." He nodded, his blond bangs sliding into his eyes.

"I bet you like school."

"Uh-huh."

Laura chuckled. Man of few words. "I'll be back down in a bit to finish up," she told Mary Grace. "Have a good day, Conner. See you later, Mary Grace."

Angel's door was shut when Laura passed it on her way to her own room. After changing into running shorts and shoes, she headed back down the hallway. As she passed Angel's room again, she paused and rapped on the door. When no one answered, she peeked inside.

"Angel?" she whispered.

"Go away," the woman growled.

Laura peered into the pitch-black room, unable to see a thing. "Can I get you something? Medicine?"

"No, I just have to wait for it to pass." Angel's voice sounded quiet and thin.

"Well, nothing to get up for. Get some rest." Laura shut the door behind her and bounded down the stairs.

She remembered her iPhone and wireless earbuds this time for her music. She was clipping the cellphone to the waistband of her shorts as Mary Grace took Connor out to her Caddy. Caleb was lucky to have her help. Laura couldn't imagine her own mother carting the grandkids around. Mama Vita had never even driven her own kids to school. The nanny did.

Laura unloaded and then reloaded the dishwasher, pressing the start button. She wiped down the counter one last time and turned off the television. The kitchen looked spotless, just as she liked it. She flipped off the lights and headed outside.

After a quick stretch, she headed down the same path she'd taken the day before.

Phyllis had certainly emerged as a different woman from what Laura had expected. She was glad, though; she had hoped one of the women could be a friend. It would get mighty lonely out here without someone to talk to, to confide in. A large green machine meandered back and forth across a nearby field, dumping what looked like corn into the back of a truck. Two men, too far away to recognize, waved at her as she jogged by.

What would have happened had Phyllis not walked into the kitchen when she had? *Nothing!* Laura's practical mind shouted. Caleb was the boss, and that was all he could be, no matter if he had lighted a long-dead flame of desire in her body.

She knew she couldn't ever tell him the real reason she was out here. Could never discuss her father's murder and the life she'd once lived. No matter how hot he was or how his eyes and attention made her feel queasy all over, they could never be a thing.

"Anhydrous tank is missing." Josh leaned back on his chair and threw his legs up on the desk in the Morning Glory office. He leaned his head back and met Caleb's eyes.

"Missing?" Caleb pushed his Pioneer seed corn hat further back on his head and scratched his forehead. "What do you mean, missing? A huge tank like that doesn't just disappear."

"I went to hook it up to the tractor and it was gone." Josh ran a hand through his hair and let his wrist rest atop his head.

"I'll be damned." Caleb tossed his cap onto his half of the desk. The tidy part. "You talk to the men? No one moved it?"

"Nope. There weren't any tire tracks, either. I just had it filled last week. I'm not sure how someone could move it without at least leaving tracks."

"I'll give Brian a call." Caleb picked up his phone and chose Brian's name from the contacts.

"You think you need the sheriff's office involved in this?"

"Damn meth addicts," Caleb swore. "Who else would take a tank of fertilizer?"

Caleb waited for the call to connect.

"Think it's safe? Especially with the new gals here?" Josh pushed his legs off the desk and stood up.

Caleb reached his buddy from high school on the first try. He explained the situation and could hear the concern in Brian's voice. When he needed more details only Josh could provide, Caleb handed the phone to his brother.

Caleb watched as Josh relayed the same story he'd given Caleb. He had not even considered the safety of the women. Laura jogging by herself.... His mom driving up here by herself.... What if someone whacked out on the junk did something crazy to them?

"Okay, Bri. We'll see ya in a bit." Josh disconnected the call and handed the phone back to Caleb.

"Just have to start locking stuff up in the buildings and make sure we lock all the doors and windows in the house at night. I'll check on the livestock more often." Caleb sat up straight.

"Easier said than done with the cattle pasturing all over the ranch now. We've got a lot more people out here than usual, and they might not be as cautious as we are."

"Two of the gals will only be here for a month, though." Caleb glanced up at the video screen that captured images from a camera monitoring the front door of the main house.

Laura was just getting back from her jog.

"A lot can happen in a month." Josh followed Caleb's line of vision and then turned to look at him again. "What happened to Angel this morning? Thought she was our breakfast cook?"

Caleb continued to stare at Laura as she did her cooldown, her shapely, toned legs stretched out in front of her. When she bent over and touched her toes, he turned away, forcing himself to focus on his brother.

"Why?"

"Well..." Josh chuckled. "The guys were hoping to get a look at her in the morning, just to see if she looks as good early as she does late."

Caleb burst into laughter. "Think she turns into a vampire or something?"

"No." Josh laughed, too.

"Someone have their eyes on her already?" Caleb hoped not. The last thing he needed was to have to pry men away from the girls to get their work done, especially now, with harvest breathing down their necks.

"Who doesn't?"

"Me," Caleb said. "And you shouldn't, either."

"I can look, can't I?" Josh flashed a sheepish grin.

"Not sure your bride would appreciate that too much."

"Well, there's Laura, too. Can't forget her. She's awful easy on the eyes."

Caleb bristled but readily agreed with Josh. Caleb was having trouble thinking of much else. He'd wanted to kiss her in the kitchen that morning, came close to doing just that, and if Phyllis hadn't bounced in when she had, he very well might have. He glanced back at the monitor. Hell, he thought, if he didn't get control, he still might kiss her.

Or even more.

At the commercial break of a documentary on President Kennedy, Caleb glanced over at his sleeping son. Connor lay sprawled out on the leather couch in their living room, exhausted and snoring softly. He'd spent the day with Laura, his new hero.

When he'd gotten home from school, Connor had planted himself on a stool in the kitchen and had demanded to bake cookies. Laura had obliged, rolling out sugar cookies for him to cut out. She'd made frosting and had found sprinkles left over from last Christmas hidden in the back of the pantry. Connor had decorated the whole batch.

Somehow, she'd made Snow White and the Seven Dwarves more interesting than Caleb ever had and had even kicked a soccer ball farther than any girl Connor had ever seen. And the smell of her ravioli at dinner had made his mouth water. She was a hell of a cook.

A soft rap on his private door drew him from his musings. It was well after ten, and Caleb expected the house to be quiet, everyone sleeping soundly like his son was. Caleb walked to the door, opened it, and found Angel on the other side.

"Hi, boss." She fluttered her eyelashes at him. "Can I talk to you?"

He held on to his laugh, amazed at her clothing choice. Wearing a shiny, satin robe and high-heeled furry slippers, there was no way in hell she was there to talk. Why the hell did she even own such a get-up?

"Sure," he answered her. "Let me put Connor in bed, and I'll meet you in the kitchen in a few minutes."

"Oh, I, uh…mean in here." She touched his shoulder and coyly met his gaze. "It's more private."

"Kitchen would be better." He retreated back into the room, shutting the door in her shocked face.

Damn, this was unwelcome. Only a few days into the cook-off challenge and already one of the women was trying to get ahead by using her body. To be hit on by a sexy lady would have flattered him years ago; now, the unwanted attention made him angry.

He covered Connor with a blanket, convinced he wouldn't be gone long, and met Angel in the kitchen. Her bare legs peeked out from under her robe as she kicked her crossed leg in the air, her heel dangling from a toe. How stupid—or gullible—did she think he was? Relieved his body was listening to his brain, he grabbed a pop from the fridge and joined her at the table.

"Feeling better?" he asked.

"Yep, I feel great right now." She flipped her long, blonde mane over her shoulder. Her look was blatant, seduction on her mind. "Since I was sick most of the day, I thought we could get to know each other tonight. Spend some time alone." She reached across the table and touched his hand.

He knew he should have sat at the center island. He pulled away and leaned fully back in his chair.

"I think we'll have plenty time to do that over the next month." He took a sip of pop, wanting to appear calmer than he felt, more in control than he was. "Don't you?"

"Aw, Caleb."

Her voice was smooth as honey, and his body tensed as she slid her chair closer, her face just inches away.

"You feel what's between us; I know you do," she whispered. "Can't we just move it along faster?" She touched his leg, rested her hand on his inner thigh, and leaned in even closer. "No one has to know."

"No." He lifted her hand off his thigh and set it on the table. "Angel," he said, getting up and moving to the counter, "when I asked you to stay away from the men on this ranch as part of the Morning Glory rules, that included me too."

"But I know you want me." She stood and walked forward, backing him into the counter and placing her hands on his shoulders.

"You misunderstood." He gently pulled her hands away. "I don't mix business and pleasure."

"What if I quit? Right this minute? Then would you consider it?" She tilted her head and licked her lips…very slowly.

"No." He dropped her hands. He wanted to laugh. Women did not usually throw themselves at him.

"Fine, then." She flipped her hair again and scowled. "I'll never stop trying, Caleb. I want you, and I know you feel the same about me."

She opened her robe, exposing the creamy flesh of her perfect breasts. He didn't take his eyes off her, curious to see if she would give him more of a show.

"You'll give in." She turned away, tossing her hair and closing her robe. "Even if it takes awhile. I think you might be worth the effort."

"You're on for breakfast at six-thirty," he called at her back, keeping his voice level.

She strolled from the kitchen, her hips deliberately swaying as she left.

"Damn." He shook his head. She had guts, he'd give her that. He turned out the lights and went back down the hall to his room. Then he did something he'd never done. He locked the main door to his wing of the house. He didn't expect her to try anything, but with people like Angel one never knew what to expect.

She had nice breasts, a nice body, but he liked to make the first move, and he never, ever dated an employee. Ever.

He walked through his living room and into the bedroom. He flipped on the light and was surprised to see three neat piles of folded laundry on his bed, his jeans pressed and his shirts ironed. Didn't take much to figure out who had taken such care. Laura had been there; he could even smell her fragrance. Maybe Angel wasn't the only one with surprises in store for him.

CHAPTER
FIVE

THE SIGHT OF ANGEL IN Caleb's arms hadn't left Laura, even after eight hours of good sleep. The night before, after relaxing on the screened-in porch with a cup of chamomile tea, Laura had passed the kitchen on her way to bed. The house had been silent when she'd gone out needing a few quiet minutes in the fresh air before hitting the hay. The last thing she'd expected to witness was a nighttime rendezvous between her boss and one of her competitors.

What bothered Laura most was that seeing them together bothered her at all. Yes, she was competitive, and the thought of someone using her body to get ahead was troubling; however, why she felt jealous over the situation she couldn't say. She had no right to feel anything at all about Caleb and his personal business. As long as he was a fair judge in the end, that was all that mattered to Laura.

She climbed from underneath the thick, down blanket and sat at the edge of the bed. Ridiculous. He was just another guy. The man who would sign her checks. With her past, that was all he could be.

Why did he have to have an adorable son, a friendly mother, and a sexy cleft in his chin? She suddenly wished he was ugly and then changed her mind.

If they had met under different circumstances, had met months ago.... If he had come to eat at Bella Vita or was one of her brother Vinny's stockbroker pals, everything would be different.

He was weak, she told herself. A typical male, succumbing to Angel's charms, her tight little butt and her big boobs. None of which Laura possessed. Well, maybe charm, but no one would call her boobs large or her ass tight. She didn't like weak men.

She stood from the bed and dressed in her running gear. These running tights were her favorite, flattered her curvy figure with their dark-purple spandex and black trim. She slipped into her running shoes and headed downstairs.

She breezed through the front door, not even bothering to check if food was cooking in the kitchen or if the sexy boss was drinking his heavy black coffee. Screw 'em. She wasn't feeling particularly charitable toward Angel or Caleb.

She stretched and darted off. About halfway down the driveway, she passed Josh going to the house. She waved but kept jogging. A parade of pickups soon followed him up the drive. Five, by Laura's count. She waved to each one as she passed, thinking that like boots and a hat, a pickup was part of the cowboy uniform. Didn't they use horses anymore?

She hit her halfway point and turned back, wondering what the day would bring. Today was a free day. She and Angel had swapped meals. Laura decided it was time to email her family via their secret accounts to let them know she was safe and make sure they were safe and settled with their fake identities and created pasts firmly set in place.

She ran the whole way back, stopping only when she tagged the porch. Male laughter drew her attention to the side of the house, where Josh and Caleb were talking. She bent over at the waist to stretch out her back and then did her cool down, walking slowly a short way up the driveway. Her lungs were burning today, and she knew she'd pushed it harder than usual. But it felt good, and through the exertion, she'd eliminated the anger, resentment, and jealousy. Or whatever she wanted to call it.

She needed this job and knew if Angel had an advantage—sexual in nature, especially—there was no way Laura could win. She might have passable looks but wasn't about to be anyone's bed buddy, not in exchange for a job. Once things cooled down with Ernesto and the gang out to get her, she could maybe settle somewhere else and open another restaurant. Or, hell, maybe she'd write that cookbook she'd been planning. But for now, she had to cool her heels and make this job work.

"Hey, Laura!" Caleb called out.

She turned, retracing her steps to the house. She forced herself to picture anything but what she had seen in the kitchen the night before.

"Morning." She smiled half-heartedly and waved. Put up a good front. "Hi, Josh!"

"Hi, yourself." Josh smiled and winked and then climbed into the driver's seat of the pickup, shutting the door.

"You seen Angel yet today?" Caleb was short, abrupt.

"No." She shook her head.

"Didn't she agree to do breakfast?" Caleb crossed his arms and leaned against the truck.

"Yeah. She said she'd cover it since I did hers yesterday."

"That's what I thought." He sighed. "Well, she didn't. No one did." He handed her a sheet of paper. "When she gets up or when you see her, give her this number and tell her to call me."

He opened the passenger side of the pickup and crawled inside. It struck her as odd that she was constantly being asked to cover for Angel—and to act as a secretary to her potential boss.

"Why not stick around and talk to her yourself?" Laura suddenly felt brave.

He stared down at her from the cab. Then he glanced at Josh.

"She's right." Josh agreed with a wide grin. "You're the boss."

Laura knew she'd like Josh.

"Feel like helping with cattle today?" Caleb slid from the cab, landing in front of her.

"Like how?" What in the hell did he have in mind?

"Just paperwork," Josh said, still grinning.

Dare she trust that smile?

"I guess. Sure."

She nodded and moved aside so Caleb could walk around her.

"Can I take a quick shower?" she asked.

Caleb laughed. "You'll be in cattle barns, Laura. They smell a hell of a lot worse than you do."

Gee, how great!

"Hop up," Josh suggested.

She walked around Caleb and hid her surprise as he helped her into the cab of the elevated pickup.

"You'll get to meet my wife, Holly," Josh told her.

"See ya." She waved to Caleb through the window.

Josh pulled out onto the driveway and headed south, back the way she'd run.

"My brother's in a state of confusion, Laura."

"How's that?"

"You women seem to be rattling his nerves."

Connor chirped away, happy to be spending the day with Caleb on the ranch. Caleb wondered how Laura was holding up with the animals. She'd had no idea what she was getting herself into. Inventory had more to it than just writing down numbers. Holly had gone down to help too, no doubt. At least she'd be comfortable chasing cows into pens. He wasn't so sure about Laura.

"I like Laura, Dad. Can we keep her?"

Caleb chuckled at the way Connor phrased his question. Caleb looked in the rearview mirror and caught his son's serious face. "I like her too, and yes, I think we'll keep her here. Maybe Phyllis too. How does that sound?"

"Real fine." The little boy nodded and looked out the window. "We're here! I see Uncle Josh's pickup too."

Caleb pulled up to the red metal Quonset hut. Inside were corrals, as well as the operation's main office. This was where he hung out most of the time. He helped Caleb out, and together they walked into the dimly lit building. Caleb paused just inside the door, waiting for his eyes to adjust to the change in light.

Laura sat on the ground, covered in dust, laughing with Holly, who was equally filthy. The cows were where they belonged in the gated area, and Caleb couldn't understand why the girls were on the ground rolling in the dirt.

"What's going on?" he demanded.

They both looked at him, stunned into silence but then burst out into greater peals of laughter. He shook his head and took Connor by the shoulder, leading him to join Josh in the office.

"What's with them, Dad?"

Caleb just shook his head. Women....

"Caleb thinks we've lost it," Holly said.

Laura had fallen on the ground after getting bowled over by a huge cow she'd tried to push through the gates. Holly had come to her rescue, managed to shove the cow away into its pen. Laura hadn't even been scared, just caught off-guard. These cows were mellow, despite being herded around by a novice cowgirl.

Laura wiped the mud from her pants as best she could and stomped her borrowed, way-too-large boots to clear off the muck.

"Let's go see what the guys need us to do next."

Still giggling like teenagers, Holly and Laura made it into the office. Laura looked around the cramped room, amazed by all that was inside. Three computers, a huge copy machine, two telephone units, and a bank of small televisions monitoring various spots on the ranch squeezed into a space the size of her old walk-in closet. Did they have cameras everywhere?

"So, how did you two end up on the ground?" Caleb asked quietly, looking down at her from his perch on a countertop.

"Yeah, Laura." Connor stood with his hands on his hips. "What were ya doing? Don't you know you're all dirty?"

Laura chuckled and bent down to look at Connor. "A cow bumped into me."

"Really?" Connor's eyes were big like saucers.

"Yep. But I'm not hurt at all, just dirty." She patted his slight shoulder and straightened again. Caleb's eyes were on her, but she looked away.

"Well." Josh hung up the phone. "Boss man says we need to get the bottom done today. He's got a truck coming tomorrow morning to pick it up."

"I thought you were the boss, Caleb?" Laura looked for a safe place to sit with the dry, dusty dirt clinging to her clothes. She leaned against the doorjamb instead, crossing her arms against her chest.

"I am. But I've got some investors. To run an operation this large, we've had to rely upon outside capital."

"Oh." She nodded. Of course, she had no idea what a ranch operation this size would cost to own and operate. "And the bottom? Where is that?"

"It's the southern border of the property. We've got it in corn, and we've been waiting 'til it was dry enough to combine it. I was planning on starting tomorrow, but like Josh said, Don, my main investor, is sending a truck to pick up the grain, so we got to get it ready or at least started today."

"Where does the truck come from?"

"You're full of questions." Caleb chuckled.

"Just curious." She shrugged and teased the hem of her jacket. Why the heck did she feel so nervous?

"Holly, let's go check how many cows we've got to load yet. Connor, you want to come?"

Josh herded them out, sidestepping Laura.

"There are a couple messages I saved for you on the machine," Josh told Caleb, hooking a thumb over his shoulder toward the phone.

Laura moved a bit further into the room. Caleb stayed on the counter, his hands resting next to his thighs.

"Did you get things straightened out with Angel?" she asked.

"Yes." He nodded. "I think so, anyway." He leaned back against the wall, crossing his arms. "She's doing dinner today."

"Thanks for letting me come out here." She laughed. "It was…different. Never in my wildest dreams did I ever think I would be chasing cows around an arena."

"I wish I could have seen you do it." He chuckled.

"I'm sure Josh can tell you what a sight it was." She laughed and pulled her hair free of the ponytail holding it back. She ran her fingers through the knotted strands, removing most of the tangles.

Blood pounded in her ears. Being this close to Caleb did crazy things to her senses. His rugged sexiness and the way he stared at her made her want to squirm. She'd never been around a man like him. Stuffy, cigar-smoking stockbrokers, yes. Shady, corrupt men, yes. Cowboys, no.

"I guess I'll go back out, up to the house."

"You don't have to." He hopped off the counter. "There's some more stuff to do out here…if you're interested?"

He walked to the opposite wall and punched a button on what looked like an intercom system.

"Hey, Caleb, it's Jenny." A woman's recorded voice sounded from the speaker. "I'll be looking for you tonight. I should be there about eight. Bye, hon."

Caleb glanced at Laura and turned back to the machine. He seemed guilty, embarrassed almost.

"This message is for Caleb. It's Amanda. Mom said you called about sitting for Connor. I'll be there about seven. Bye."

The machine beeped twice, and then the room fell silent. Apparently, there were no more messages. So…Caleb was going on a date with Jenny and a girl named Amanda would be babysitting Connor tonight. So what? She couldn't let herself care.

"We are going to town tonight," Caleb said, explaining the obvious. "The boys usually go on Friday and Saturday. One of the bars in town tries to get a band on Fridays."

"Sounds like fun." She couldn't think of anything else to say.

"You're welcome to come too."

"Sounds more like Angel's speed than mine," she said. "I'll tell them, though."

She walked to the door and opened it. He grabbed her arm and turned her toward him. Sparks of heat shot through the fabric of her running suit, and she looked into his eyes. Did he feel the same—that instant physical attraction? She lifted a questioning brow.

"What will you do instead?" He whispered the question.

Could he sense her attraction? Were her cheeks as red as she thought they were? She felt warm all over.

"Read a book, probably. Maybe watch a movie. I like your satellite system." She smiled at him, wishing her heart would quit pounding so hard. Could he hear it? "It's been a long time since I had a Friday night to myself."

"Big social life in Chicago?"

She could hear the sneer in his voice, even if his face remained expressionless.

"Hardly," she scoffed. "I cooked on Friday nights. And Saturdays. I haven't had a true social life since college."

He let go of her arm. "If you change your mind, you're welcome to come along."

"Thanks." She turned back after walking partway through the door. She didn't want to leave him, but she also remembered the vision of him with Angel the night before. Angel had staked her claim. "When will you have the next schedule posted?"

"The guys will vote after dinner tonight." He shoved his hands in the pockets of his tight, hip-hugging jeans. "Top vote gets the weekend off."

"I'll be more patient," she said. "See ya."

She waggled her fingers at him and walked out the door, fighting the urge to look back, to stay for just a few more minutes.

On the short trek back to the main house, she decided two things. One, she would not let him get to her, and two, he was just another sexy cowboy.

If she truly believed either, pigs would be flying in the eastern sky by morning.

45

CHAPTER
SIX

"L AURA, CAN I TALK TO you for a minute?" Angel was watching a soap opera in the living room when Laura returned from her adventure with the cows.

"Sure." Laura joined her at the fireplace, curious and a little guarded. She didn't trust the other woman.

"I wanted to apologize to you for not doing my share," Angel said, "for not following the schedule and making you and Phyllis pick up the slack."

Caleb must have chewed her ass. Laura bit her lip to avoid laughing at the fake look of remorse on Angel's face. So, what was the catch? Laura wasn't buying the apology, not for a minute, but she decided it might be fun to play along.

"I am just so happy you're up and about." Laura played her role as a concerned friend. "Phyllis and I were worried about you." She screwed up her face into a look of true concern.

"Things are looking up," Angel said. "I think I have a pretty good chance of winning this competition now."

Laura knew exactly what Angel was referring to—the romantic interlude with Caleb the night before. Had Caleb really fallen for Angel's ploy? Laura knew Caleb was headed out for an evening with someone named Jenny. Laura doubted Angel knew about that.

Laura held out her hand. "Let the best woman win."

Angel shook hands, a fake smile turning up her heavily glossed lips. "I hope you have a back-up plan, Laura. I would hate to see you homeless."

Laura dropped her hand and turned to leave, no quick quip coming to mind.

"You're making lunch, right?" Angel called out.

"Yep, that's the plan," Laura answered.

"We'll see you then," Angel called.

Laura trailed up to her room, in need of a shower and a change of clothing. The taste of dirt from the cattle barn still lingered in her mouth. At least Holly had been fun, and Josh was as laid-back as a person could be. If only Caleb was as easy to understand as his brother was.

"Laura!" Caleb walked into the house yelling for her, and she was quick to respond, as she was only a few feet from the front door.

"I'm in the kitchen."

"Maybe he'll know where everyone is for supper," Phyllis said. Phyllis and Laura had been waiting for the men for almost a half hour. "It'll be cold by the time they show up," Phyllis added.

Caleb enter the kitchen. "Hi, Phyllis." He turned toward Laura. "Can I talk to you in the living room for a minute, please?"

"Sure." She exchanged a worried glance with Phyllis, and then followed the boss out of the kitchen, back to where she and Angel had visited earlier. When they were alone, she asked, "What's the matter?"

"What exactly did you put in lunch today?" Caleb towered over her, his hands balled on his hips.

"What do you mean?" She hated to be on guard. "It was just plain chili and grilled cheese."

"Did you use some weird spices?"

"No." She shook her head, struggling to remember what combination of seasonings she had used. "Not at all. In fact, I went light on the spices because I wasn't sure how hot your guys like it."

"They like it spicy," Caleb said. "But unfortunately, there was something in it that has kept them in the bathroom all day. None of them has been out of it long enough to get anything done. Whatever you put in there made them sick, Laura! I can't afford to have all my men too ill to work. You hear me?"

"You're shouting at me, Caleb. Of course, I can hear you." She sank onto the nearest chair, stunned. "I didn't do anything out of the ordinary. I cooked the burger long enough. What could have made everyone sick?"

"I have no idea, but you damn well need to figure it out, so it never happens again."

Caleb stalked from the room, leaving her sitting in stunned silence.

Laura could hear him telling Phyllis to pack up the dinner because the men wouldn't be leaving the comforts of their beds tonight. Blinking back the tears stinging her eyes, Laura left the living room for the privacy of her room.

Angel, dressed for a night out, met Laura halfway down the stairs.

"I heard yelling," Angel said. "Is everything okay?"

"Sure, just fine." Laura blinked fast to clear the tears from her eyes. "Well, except all the men are ill and can't go party with you in town tonight."

"You're kidding, right?" Angel looked crestfallen.

"Caleb said no one is going tonight. I guess there was something in the chili that didn't agree with them." Laura brushed past Angel. "See you tomorrow."

Laura slammed the door to her room, glad Caleb had the heavy kind of doors that made a firm thud when they were slammed. She kicked off her shoes and then flopped onto her bed. How the hell had her cooking made anyone sick?

She was fine, and she'd eaten some. Phyllis wasn't sick, either. Only the men had gotten sick, although, Caleb looked fine, and he'd eaten his share, too. Were they all sick or just a few of them? She considered the spices she used again. Just the usual ones—chili powder, cayenne pepper, black pepper, salt. The meat had been completely fried before she even added it to the tomatoes. She wanted to crawl under the blankets and hide. Nothing more embarrassing to a cook than making people sick.

Her laptop, resting on the table in the corner of the room, dinged, letting her know she had a new email waiting for her. Curious and feeling lonely for her family, her support system, she stood and went to see who was contacting her.

An email from her sister and a few spam emails were in her inbox. She deleted the junk and opened the note from her sister, Maria, now known as Liz, a former teacher of high school kids in the inner-city.

Watch your back, Bre, she wrote, forgetting to call her Laura. *They found Vinny. Careless idiot was still using his credit cards. I love and miss you. M.*

"The news today just gets better and better."

Laura flopped back onto the bed, switched on the TV to the Travel Channel, and wished she could be anywhere but where she was at the moment—even in the haunted, Scottish manor house some pretty blonde British chick was exploring.

Phyllis won the first round of the cook-off. The guys hadn't had a hard time picking the winner, seeing as Angel had been absent most of her scheduled meals and Laura's chili had made everyone sick. Having the ladies out there was definitely bringing more excitement to the place, but Caleb was still spending another boring Friday night in front of the TV.

"Hi, Caleb."

Laura's voice from the doorway surprised him, and he turned to see her.

"You probably aren't too excited to see me right now, huh?" She leaned her hip against the back of the couch, facing the fireplace. "Sorry if your plans were ruined for the evening."

She looked like she had been crying; her eyes were red rimmed and looked puffy in the light. He'd been too hard on her, probably. Her other meals had been terrific, and she had a work ethic he didn't often encounter—even when she was pushing around cows that weighed five times more than she did.

"I don't believe you set out to make the guys sick." He flipped off the television and motioned for her to sit.

She sniffed and shook her head. "I'm headed to the kitchen to see the ingredients I used. I want to double check that I didn't grab something odd without realizing."

"I'll come with you." He tossed the TV remote on the couch and stood up. "Maybe together we can figure it out?"

Laura went straight to the pantry and came out carrying a few small spice containers.

"I'll check if there's anything out of the ordinary in there." He went inside the small room but couldn't see anything unusual on the shelves, certainly nothing that would cause someone to get ill.

He joined her again in the kitchen, empty-handed, and watched silently as she studied the petite containers, checking their dates and smelling them.

"Do you have any of the ground beef left?"

She pointed him to the stainless-steel fridge. "It's in the meat keeper, in a zip baggie."

To the naked eye, it looked fine, and even after he opened it and smelled it, it seemed perfectly usable. "Is this the leftover chili in here? In the plastic sealed container?"

She got off her stool and looked over his shoulder into the fridge. "Yeah, that's it."

He pulled it out and took it to the counter. Opening it, he immediately noticed an odd smell. He brought the bowl closer to his nose and then farther away, frowning.

"What do you smell?"

He pushed the container toward her nose, and she ducked her head to get closer.

"Eww," she said. "Is that peppermint?"

He put the plastic container down and walked toward the dining room.

"Where are you going?" she called from behind.

"Come with me." He looked at her over his shoulder. "I have an idea."

He walked through the vacant dining room and into the bathroom used by the staff. He slid open the medicine cabinet, not at all surprised to find the laxatives missing. The cabinet was always stocked with the usual pain relievers, sore muscle gels, stomach ache pills, and probably as recently as this morning, there'd been laxatives in there too.

"Well?" Laura stood behind him, her hands shoved in the pockets of her jeans.

"It would appear someone added the peppermint-flavored laxatives to your stew. They're missing, and that's what I smelled in the chili when I open the container."

"Who would do that?"

He stared at her, marveling at her naiveté. "Considering you're competing for this job, I guess there could be a number of choices."

"But I'm not the one suffering; your men are." She walked back into the kitchen and slumped onto a chair. "How will we know who did it?"

"Good question." He joined her at the table. "Who had access to the kitchen all alone today?"

They both considered the question.

"I was with Holly at the barn until eleven. Anyone could have slipped something in the pan. Really anyone who had been in the kitchen anytime today could have done it. If they had the idea, had a plan, all they'd need is a few minutes alone, I would guess."

"Who was here when you got back?"

"Phyllis was working in the laundry room." Laura dropped her head into her hands. "I can't imagine she would do something so mean. She's a good cook in her own right, a nice lady."

"You saying I should hire her?"

Laura's head popped up. "I would rather you didn't."

He chuckled at her fast reaction. "Any men hanging around?" Caleb asked. "I think they were supposed to be out on the field, getting the harvest set, but one could have snuck in here."

"Were there any men who *didn't* get sick?"

"Nope. Josh said they all were. They all ate. Josh, too, I'm afraid."

"I'm not sick," Laura said. She motioned his way. "You're not sick. Phyllis and Angel are fine. We all ate it."

"But we ate out of the pot in the kitchen, not the dishes and the dining room."

"Right." She agreed with a nod. "So someone had to slip it into the pot in the dining room?"

"Would appear so, yes."

Laura left the room a few minutes later, having gathered as much information as they would get at the moment. What else could be said? Someone was out to get the Morning Glory, and things just seemed to be getting worse. Missing fertilizer from the week before and now poisoned chili. Any more disasters and they'd have a serious crisis on their hands.

CHAPTER

SEVEN

CALEB WAS ON A MISSION to get laid.

Determined to get the problems of the ranch and Laura's sad face out of his mind, he rescheduled his date with Jenny, the good time girl. She'd work her special magic and remove Laura from his head and his blood. Jenny knew there wouldn't be anything beyond the sex—there never was. They enjoyed each other's company once in a while. Convenience without commitment and no complications. That's how they both liked it.

He parked his truck in a stall and did a final check of his hair and shave job in the rearview mirror. The sitter had been late, and by the time she'd gotten there, Con didn't want to be left home alone with her. It was too late for Caleb to worry about it. Besides, Amanda was a nice girl—her family farmed down the road a couple of miles—and she would make sure his son was entertained for the evening. Con would be fine; he just wasn't accustomed to Caleb leaving him and Amanda babysitting.

Both Phyllis and Angel had decided to come along but rode in a separate vehicle with some of the farmhands who were now back to their old selves, looking forward to downing a few beers to wash away any remnants of pain. One guy had been left on duty. Caleb always had someone at the ranch.

Phyllis looked completely different from the day she arrived at the ranch. Pretty, even. She'd put her hair up in a fancy style, had tasteful make-up on, and had even donned a low-cut T-shirt and form-fitting jeans. She looked younger, and while she didn't look particularly comfortable, she looked happy.

Angel, on the other hand, was completely in her element—a small-town bar with small-town boys—looking for a good time. Without question, she was sexy and any guy looking for a good time could probably find it with her. Her miniskirt barely covered her ass, and her silky blouse was cut lower than was decent and only covered one shoulder. She wore high-heeled boots and looked more like a stripper than a cook.

He stepped out of the pickup, satisfied with the shine of his boots and the crease in his jeans. The street in front of the bar was packed; he'd been forced to park half a block down the road. He waved as a pickup filled with his ranch hands drove by. They could drink all they wanted in town, but they couldn't take any booze back to the ranch. They all understood what the result would be if they did. Caleb had seen firsthand what alcohol and drugs could do to a person, and he was not about to lose all he had built because men couldn't keep their heads screwed on straight.

He walked into the bar, shook the hand of the bouncer, and paid the band's cover charge. He spotted Jenny and ambled his way to the table where she sat with other men from the Morning Glory. He slowed his pace, moving with confidence.

"Hey, Jenny." He pulled out a chair next to her. "You look great."

"Thanks, hon." Everyone was *hon* to her—or babe. Even if she didn't know a person. She did hair in town, waited tables on the weekends. She reveled in knowing everyone's business, knew the gossip, who was cheating on who, who was getting fired or was about ready to quit. He'd learned to be on guard when he spoke to her, part of the reason he could never have anything more with her than a casual relationship.

"Can I get you something?" He angled his neck toward the bar.

"Sure, babe." Jenny nodded and tilted an already-empty brown bottle toward him. "Another Lite would be great."

He stood and made his way back through the throng of people. After he ordered, he turned back to survey the crowd. He nodded to a couple of men he recognized. One he'd gone to school with, the other, Jasper, owned a nearby ranch more than double the size of Caleb's.

He took Jenny's beer and his pop and went back to where she sat working the table. She loved the attention of the cowboys. She reminded him a lot of Christie, another reason they would never get any further than where they were.

"Wanna dance, hon?" Jenny put a hand on his upper thigh as if it were the most natural thing to do.

"Not tonight." He shook his head and took a sip of pop.

The band was cranking up. Lucky for the boys, the band had a two-night stand at the bar and their sickness the night before wasn't preventing their partying. It was a good old-fashioned country band, a group that had been in town many times before.

"I'll swing ya 'round." Will, one of Morning Glory's longtime employees, took her hand, and away she went, not even bothering to ask if Caleb cared.

"So, what's new?" Jasper smacked Caleb on the back and took over the chair Jenny had vacated.

"Not much." Caleb shook his head. "Well, I guess something's new." He leaned his chair on the back two legs. "Stella quit. Juan's been having pains in his gut, and the docs think it might be his liver." He swallowed. "They're up at Mayo getting some tests run."

"Really? Too much of this, I suppose?" Jasper tilted his beer bottle toward Caleb.

"I don't know for sure." Caleb spoke loud enough to be heard over the music.

He studied Jenny as she floated around on the floor with Will. Caleb wasn't jealous, more like annoyed. He had no claim on her, but good manners dictated she at least not flirt with every other man in the bar while they were out together.

"So, did you find someone to take her place?"

Caleb nodded. "I brought out three gals, thought it would be kind of fun to have them compete for the job. One came all the way from Chicago."

"No shit?"

Caleb laughed. "I hired a couple of new hands too." He nodded at the neighboring table. "That's one of them, and the blonde is one of the cooks I'm trying out."

"Hell, Caleb, she'll never work out." Jasper leaned forward; it was getting even louder in the bar. "All the men will fantasize about gettin' in her pants."

"Yeah, I know."

"You too?" Jasper laughed and about choked on his beer.

"No." Caleb shook his head. "It's the one from Chicago who's got me going."

"Is she here?" Jasper looked around. "So many people tonight, wouldn't even notice a new person."

"Naw, she decided to stay at the ranch," Caleb answered. "She's pretty fine too."

"What about the third gal?"

"She's over at the bar, talking with Wendy."

"She's not bad, either. Pretty smile," Jasper told him, while staring at Phyllis. "You lucky son of a—

"Hey, now." Caleb chuckled. "It's more pain than it's worth."

"Wish I had that kind of ache." Jasper winked. "I got the harvesting done last night, by the way. Noticed you've got a lot of corn still standing."

"Yeah, yeah." Caleb rolled his eyes at his friend. It was an ongoing competition between the two of them.

"You plan to go to the Cattleman's Association deal again this year?"

"Sure." Caleb nodded. "I'll drive this time. I guess I owe ya."

"They're doing some fancy dinner dance thing this year." Jasper stood up as Jenny walked back to the table. "I'll probably bring a date along."

"Oh, yeah?" That interested Caleb. Jasper was years older than Caleb, never married, and as far as Caleb knew, never had any intention of getting hitched.

"Yeah. I just have to find her first. Maybe I'll go talk to your cook at the bar." Jasper patted Caleb's shoulder. "What's her name?"

Caleb told him.

"Huh. She doesn't look like a Phyllis. Hey, Jenny." Jasper tipped his cowboy hat. "I'll call you next week about the conference."

Caleb watched him walk to the bar and sit next to Phyllis. He must have said he knew Caleb, because she looked over at him. Caleb nodded and winked. Jasper was a good guy and got her to dance with him. Maybe she wasn't the quiet mouse Caleb had thought she was.

"So, Caleb." Jenny placed her hand back on his thigh. "What's kickin'?"

"Not a whole lot." Caleb shrugged and leaned back in his chair, stretching his legs out in front of him under the table. "Just wanted to see you, that's all."

"Is that one of your new cooks? The blonde hanging on the guy over there?"

Jenny pointed at Angel, and Caleb nodded.

"Jasper's dancing with the other one."

"I thought you had *three* new gals competing? Where's the other one?" Jenny scanned the crowd.

"Yeah, Laura stayed back at the ranch."

"Not a partier, huh?" Jenny sipped her beer.

"I think she could hold her own." Caleb gave in to an odd compulsion to defend her.

"Hit a sore spot, did I?" Jenny rubbed up his thigh. Some nights, that's all it would have taken to get him to leave a tip at the table and hit the road to find a private place to fool around. Tonight, her touch just annoyed him. Like her fake-baked skin, thick makeup, and the stale scent of cigarettes that clung to her.

"No," he smoothly lied, removing her hand from his lap. "Not at all. You're probably right; she's more of a homebody." Looking around the bar, watching people make fools out of themselves, Caleb realized he'd much rather be back at the ranch himself.

"I heard Jasper mention the Beef Ball. Don't suppose you'd like me to come along?" She leaned in close and laughed. "I clean up pretty good."

"Yes, you do." The thought of taking her, even being with her tonight, made him feel dirty. He'd come to get laid but realized he couldn't. He felt disgusted with himself that he'd planned such a stupid thing.

"Babe, what's on your mind?" She looked genuinely concerned.

"Nothing. I'm just not much in the mood to be here tonight, I guess. Sorry I'm not better company." He sipped on his pop.

"In that case, I'll just make myself happy." She winked. "Watch this." She stood up and sashayed to the table where Angel sat with Paul, the new ranch hand.

Jenny bent and whispered something in Paul's ear, and he smiled. She took his hand, and off to the dance floor they went. The band was kicking up a fast song, and Caleb mentally wished Paul well as he tried to keep up with Jenny. Angel was shooting Jenny dirty looks, and Caleb worried she would be over at his table soon, trying to make her own point.

He leaned back on his chair and watched the other people having fun. Drinking too much liquor. The band was good, people were dancing—some badly. Why was he thinking about Laura? What did it matter what she was doing? She'd told him she'd be reading or maybe watching television. End of story.

But it wasn't.

There were so many complexities to the woman from Chicago. Maybe she fascinated him because she came from such a different background? Sure, she was pretty, but as he looked around the packed bar, he saw other women just as good-looking. Maybe it was her smile? Remembering her rolling in the dirt? He chuckled to himself. Who was to say what the reason was? After three short days, he was hooked.

And he sure as hell didn't want to be.

"Laura!"

A tugging, shaking of her shoulder jolted her awake. Where the hell was she?

"Caleb," she breathed and slowly sat up on the couch.

"What's going on?" The harshness of his voice made her jump. "Why are you in here, and where is Amanda?"

She looked around the dimly lit room, still in a sleep-induced haze. She ran her hand over her face and through her hair. Then she remembered where she was. And why.

"Connor had an accident in his bed," she whispered, knowing the little boy was only a short distance away, sleeping.

"I see," Caleb said. "But that doesn't explain how you came to be here and not Amanda."

"Can you turn on another light, maybe?" Laura yawned and dropped her legs off the side of the couch.

He obliged, choosing the lowest setting.

"He must have had a dream and didn't quite make it to the bathroom in time," Laura said. "I was sitting on the porch again and heard Amanda yelling. I thought there was a burglar or something, so I came in to see what was going on. Anyway, her yelling made Connor feel worse. She was really mad about it, and it's a shame because Connor was still half asleep. Like me." She grinned. "But the sitter freaked out. He said she spanked him, but I didn't bother to ask her. I just told her she could go home, that I would take care of him until you got here."

"So, is he in his bed?"

"Yes." She nodded and yawned again. "We found new jammies and sheets. I made up the bed and rocked with him for a little while, told him a story, and he went right back to sleep."

"Thank you." He shoved his hands back into his pockets.

"No problem." She stood up and grabbed the arm of the couch, still feeling groggy and little fuzzy from sleep. "Did you have a nice night?"

"It was fine," he answered without much conviction in his voice.

She glanced at the clock, surprised it was so early, just after eleven. She felt like she had slept longer than an hour.

"You smell like cigarettes."

She wrinkled her nose.

"I hate that stale smell."

"Must be from the bar. I don't smoke," he told her.

"Pop smoked cigars, but no one else in the family did."

"What about alcohol?"

"Yeah, he drank quite a bit too." She nodded, remembering the calls at three in the morning after one of his poker games when he was too drunk to get home by himself.

"I meant you, Laura."

"Oh!" She laughed. "Nothing with any regularity."

"Sex?"

Did he just ask that? "What was that?" she squeaked.

"You heard me." He laughed. "Do you have sex?"

"I have," she said, feeling the need for honesty in this ridiculous and uncomfortable conversation. "I haven't for some time."

"Me either." He walked to her, stopping only a few feet in front of her. "Tell me why you're out here, Laura. The only places I've had food like you cook is at four-star restaurants. Kansas City and Omaha—the big cities. Why waste your talent out here on us?"

He towered over her but didn't intimidate her. How to answer that? She'd known someone would ask her. She wished she were better prepared with a legitimate response. She took a minute before replying.

"I needed a change. Pop died, and I knew if I didn't start living now, I never would."

She watched him stare at her. When his eyes focused on her lips, she had an idea of what was going through his mind, making her heart flutter. She found herself backing away and bumping into the doorjamb.

His gaze locked on hers, making her body ache for his touch, even the slightest brush of his fingertips. She swallowed, wanting to move toward him but knowing what it would lead to was wrong. He made the first move, but she ducked, a sudden vision of him and the nearly naked Angel canoodling in the kitchen serving as a bucket of cold water to her senses.

Laura backed farther away from him, hightailing it before she did something stupid. "Night, boss man." She fled like a coward through the door, afraid of the attraction.

CHAPTER

EIGHT

JUST AS HE WAS TURNING out the light, Caleb found a pair of glasses on the closed laptop sitting next to his recliner. Laura wore glasses? Could he dampen down his hormones enough to deliver them to her tonight?

After changing from his smoke-scented jeans and shirt into sweats, he left the comfort of his private room and went down the hallway, carrying the laptop and her glasses. As he reached the stair landing, loud music assaulted his ears. Following the noise like the lines on a map, he ended up outside Angel's room.

Ignoring the noise—it was Angel's ears, not his—he walked to the end of the hall. Phyllis's room was dark, her door wide open. Laura's door was closed and silent as he leaned his ear against the wood. She was probably back asleep. He rapped once, wondering how she could possibly sleep with the racket at the other end of the hall.

When she didn't answer, he tried the door, and it clicked open. A lamp burned low next to the bed, lighting the room in a soft glow. Laura was lying on her side, facing away from the door. Caleb set the laptop and glasses on the table by the door and then walked quietly to the bed and touched her shoulder. She flipped toward him, her eyes wide with the surprise.

"What's wrong?" she asked and pulled a set of headphones off her ears. He could hear strands of classical music before she paused it.

"I'm sorry," Caleb said. "I shouldn't have tried to kiss you."

"You did?" she asked, a confused look on her face.

"You know damn well I was going to." He sat on the edge of the bed and then changed his mind and stood up again. "I think it's better that I… that we didn't…"

"Because you spent the evening with Jenny?" Laura chuckled. "Or is it because you're already getting what you need from Angel?"

"Come again?"

"You spent the—"

"Wait. Wait." He held up both hands to stop her. "Yes, I was with Jenny. Not exactly *with* Jenny But what are you implying about Angel?"

"I saw you in the kitchen with her, Caleb. She was dressed in a flimsy, slinky robe thingy, and you were all over her. I'm not blind."

"Stop already." He chuckled. Hell, Laura was jealous. "She was trying to get on my good side."

"Whatever." Laura sighed.

He could tell she wasn't buying it. Recalling what happened in the kitchen, he imagined she'd caught an eyeful.

"What do you need from me now? Can I not get some sleep?"

"Sure." Calling himself ten times an idiot, he nodded. He should have just waited until the morning to see her. He pointed to the table where he had set the laptop and glasses. "I thought you might need them."

"You couldn't have just set them on the table for me and left?"

Of course, he could have. How dumb of him not to. He didn't answer her.

She lifted her earphones up off her lap. "On your way out, would you ask Angel to lower the volume? Or maybe have her take the party elsewhere?"

"Will do."

He watched quietly as she put her headphones back on. She turned her back on him and cuddled back into the bed, just as she was when he'd entered. He wanted to climb in behind her; it was almost midnight, and he was tired.

Closing the door quietly, he steeled his courage to face Angel again. He didn't need to listen too closely at the door to hear male laughter. "Damn." That was the last thing he wanted to deal with.

He banged on the door loudly enough to be heard. Laura had music and her headphones, Phyllis was still out, and Con was too far away to hear, so he pounded away. When the music didn't quiet, he tried the door but found it locked.

"Angel, shut the music off now!" he screamed.

The music ended abruptly, and even through the door Caleb could hear the wrestling of sheets and curses.

He pounded the door again. "Who's in there with you?"

More curses and giggles. Caleb had a good idea who would be sharing her bed. When he'd left the bar, she and Paul had been making out in a dark corner booth. The man had practically been under her skirt even then.

The door opened and Paul stepped out, not meeting Caleb's eyes. Paul carried his boots under an arm while buttoning up his shirt. Glancing inside, Caleb could see Angel holding something behind her back, having trouble standing up without swaying.

"What's behind your back?" he demanded.

She produced a half-empty bottle of vodka and giggled. "Guess we're busted."

"I hope it was worth it," Caleb grumbled. "You're both fired. I would have let you off with a warning if it was just the sex part, but no way with the liquor."

"Aww." Angel shimmed up to Caleb. "You jealous, baby? You want a little lovin' too?"

Caleb rolled his eyes and stepped back into the hallway to avoid the smell of the vodka. "Pack your bags. Both of you. You'll get a free ride to town tonight. You've got an hour to pack."

Angel slammed the door in Caleb's face; Paul just turned on his heel and walked downstairs, holding the rail tightly as he went.

"Aw, hell." Caleb shoved a hand through his hair. He was going to have to wake Laura again. She'd have to watch Connor. Phyllis wasn't home yet, and Caleb was not going to wake up his six-year-old in the middle of the night to cart off two horny drunks. Maybe he'd just wait until the morning and have Josh take them home. He sure didn't want to be driving around in the middle of the night. He would, however, haul them back to town and get them a hotel room for what was left of the night.

Sighing, he went back to Laura's room, hoping she wouldn't end up quitting because of this fiasco.

"How many times did you wake up that poor girl?" His mother asked Caleb. She'd come up for the morning after hearing about the troubles at the ranch when she filled up her gas tank in town.

"What could I do? I couldn't just let her sleep on the couch." Caleb sipped from his mug and sighed.

"Just think. Had you let her be, then you wouldn't have found Angel and the guy." She leaned against the counter and tilted her head. "You would have gotten all your sleep and wouldn't be so irritable this morning." She fluffed her high hair and refilled her coffee cup. "I'd maybe be eating something wonderful instead of these stale donuts. Where is she now? Laura, I mean."

"My bed." He grinned and choked on the coffee when Mom slapped his back.

"Very funny. Ha, ha." She sat in her usual spot at the table. "You slept in her room then?"

"Yep," he answered.

"Good morning!" Josh breezed into the kitchen, holding Holly's hand. He kissed their mom on the cheek and plopped himself down at the table, pulling Holly onto his lap.

Caleb hadn't seen them the night before in town; they usually came to the bar when a band was playing.

"Hate to burst your bubble of happiness." Caleb chuckled. "I need you to return Angel and Paul to their homes."

"What happened?" Holly asked.

Everyone knew about the ranch rules, so it would be an easy story to tell. Caleb filled them in and even included Laura's involvement.

"They didn't even last a week." Josh shook his head. "That Paul was a good worker."

Caleb thought about it as he sipped on his coffee. "Maybe you could drop Angel off first, then just bring Paul back. Give him a stiff warning about the alcohol and such?"

"That's not fair!" Holly said. "Why keep the guy and not the cook? They were equally guilty."

"We have two really good cooks," Caleb told her, "but we need more ranch hands."

"But Laura got all the men sick. You're keeping her and getting rid of Angel just because she sleeps with guys?"

"I don't think Laura did it," Caleb answered. "Someone else doctored up the lunch with laxatives. I have a pretty good idea that it was the person I canned last night."

"Angel?" Josh asked.

"Yeah. I found the laxatives in the chili."

"Laxatives? Well, I'll be damned. I suppose the chili disguised the flavor." Josh sighed. "That would have worked. Not sure why you think it was Angel though."

"Got my reasons," Caleb said. "Laura and Phyllis will do just fine."

"Paul was fitting in real good with the other guys. I liked him." Josh winked at Holly. "On a different topic. We've got some news to share."

"Good news, I hope. After last night, I've had enough bad for a while," Caleb grumbled.

"Holly's expecting," Josh said quietly, a grin threatening to split his face into two.

"As I live and breathe!" Mom was up and out of her seat. She kissed Holly first and then threw her arms around them both. "How far along?"

"I think about three months already." Holly flushed. "Just wanted to be sure before we told you."

"Congratulations." Caleb smiled.

Christie's news about Connor hadn't been a particularly happy event. She and Caleb hadn't been married, and she hadn't been interested in getting hitched—baby or no baby. But Caleb loved Connor the minute he was born and committed himself to do anything to make him safe and happy. He was proud of the dad he'd become, proud of the son he was raising.

"Did I miss something?" Laura stepped into the kitchen with her usual beautiful smile.

Caleb caught his breath and swallowed.

Purple suited her, brought out the blue in her eyes. She had her dark hair down this morning, and it laid in waves about her shoulders. She had on makeup too, which was uncommon for her in the morning. She wasn't wearing a running outfit either. Instead, she had on a pair of jeans that looked as if they'd been custom made for her.

"I'm pregnant." Holly smiled.

"Oh, how wonderful!" Laura told them, her smile getting even larger. "Congratulations to you both." She smiled at his mother. "Hi, Mary Grace."

"Surprised you're up already," Mom said. "Caleb filled me in on what happened last night."

"It was a long one, that's for sure." She poured herself a cup of coffee and added a bit of milk and sugar. "Holly, you probably shouldn't have been rolling around in the dirt with me the other day."

"What's that?" Mom asked, making both men groan.

"They helped me cull down in the barn, so we could get the younger ones tagged before calving and the cold comes," Josh told his mom. "Holly, let's head out; we've got a good six hours on the road today."

"In the party van?" Laura asked with a laugh.

Caleb shot a look her way and was delighted by the laughing twinkle he saw. She had been humored by her mode of transportation to the ranch—as cheesy as it may have been.

"Nope. Had to take that back. Someone might be riding in it right now, as a matter of fact. It was reserved for a wedding in Scottsbluff for yesterday." Josh put his mug in the sink.

"Angel and Paul are at Sally Baker's in town. They're expecting you," Caleb informed them.

"Okay." Josh slipped an arm around Holly and guided her out. "You know where to find us. I'll answer the cell this time, should you happen to call." He saluted Caleb and went out. "Bye, Mom." The screen door slammed shut behind them.

"So, what have you got planned today?" Mom asked Caleb.

"The trucker never made it yesterday to pick up the grain. Don called to say he'd be out this morning. I should be out at the bins to watch him load it."

"Sounds like fun." Her voice held a sarcastic edge. "Will you take Connor out there or should I snag him home for the rest of the weekend?"

"Could." He nodded. "I'll ask and see what he wants to do."

"And you, Laura. What's going on with you?"

"Lunch duty." She shrugged. "I should write some emails. Nothing too exciting. Maybe I'll even take a nap today."

She laughed, and he wondered if it was because she never napped or because it was so obvious they all needed one?

Connor entered the kitchen and plowed into Caleb's hip. "You want to go watch them load the corn or you want to hang out with Grandma today?"

"What about Laura?" He whispered the question, but his voice was still loud enough for all three of the adults to hear him.

"What about me?" She leaned closer to him.

The little boy flushed and turned his head and to his dad's hip. "Can we make more cookies today?" His voice was muffled.

"Sure," Laura readily agreed with a laugh. "But maybe Grandma wants to spend the day with you?"

"Maybe I'll just stay out here and help bake cookies?" Mom said. "We'll make some extras for Grandpa Hank."

"How about you go and get dressed while I figure out what to make for lunch?" Laura said. "I'll come get you in a bit, okay?"

"Okey-dokey." Connor scampered off.

"You don't have to, you know. This isn't part of the job description," Caleb said.

"I know, but I don't mind," Laura answered.

"He needs a woman's touch, Caleb," Mom said.

"He's got you."

"Yes, but I'm Grandma. I'm an old lady. Laura here is full of energy. Have you seen her run? Those beautiful legs of hers?"

Laura flushed. Caleb was sure his mouth was hanging open. His mother never quit. Was she matchmaking or was it his imagination?

Too bad he'd sworn off women.

CHAPTER
NINE

Feeling Caleb's eyes on her, Laura looked up from her laptop and found him staring at her.

"What?" she asked.

They'd been sitting in companionable silence at the kitchen table for almost an hour. He was waiting for the truck driver to show up, killing time reading *Farm and Ranch* magazine while she worked on her computer, looking for more breakfast dishes the men might like and checking e-mails. A small television was on a news channel in the background, but she wasn't really listening to it. Connor had finally gone to take a nap, and the lunch dishes were cleaned and put away.

"Just wondered what you were looking at. You've been laughing and not sharing." He took a sip of pop. "I call that rude."

"Just reading emails from my family." She shrugged, not feeling rude at all.

"Tell me about them." He closed his magazine and leaned back in his chair, stretching out his long, muscular legs under the table.

This was the moment she'd been dreading since she'd landed on the Morning Glory's doorstep. What could she safely say about her family? How much could she reveal without worry? Did he really care or was he just trying to fill the long moments of silence? She could make up some story about a happy, *normal* Chicago family, but she'd probably eventually forget the details.

"Why?" Laura pushed her chair back and stood, intent on grabbing one of the freshly baked chocolate chip cookies from the plate on the counter.

Caleb snagged her arm as she tried to walk past. "I want to know."

He was serious. Almost too serious, but that didn't prevent warmth of his hand from penetrating her sleeve, running the length of her arm. Desire. Lust. That was all it was. She wanted him, had felt the powerful pull when she met him that very first night.

"Okay." She nodded and pulled away gently, so as not to offend him.

She kinda liked him holding her, even if it was only her arm. She picked up the plate of cookies, brought it to the table, and set it down in front of him. She sat again, and after pouring them each a glass of milk, she put her feet up on a chair under the table, stretching out her legs. She pushed a cookie toward him. "Tit for tat." She broke a cookie in half and dunked it in the glass.

"What does that mean, exactly?" His face scrunched up, questioning.

"So, you ask a question, I answer. I ask, then you answer."

"Deal." He nodded. "I go first."

"What about ladies first?" She chuckled.

"It's my house." He shrugged.

She snorted. "It's my house." She imitated his voice and snorted again.

"Why did you leave Chicago?"

"I answered that last night," she said, biting into the other half of the cookie. "When you woke me up the *first* time." She frowned. "Didn't I?"

"Yeah." He munched on the cookie. "But I don't believe you."

"Well." She swallowed, meeting his gaze with her own. "It's true. I wanted to explore life beyond the lake."

He looked at her hard, and she was pretty sure he still wasn't buying what she was saying.

"What kind of restaurant were you working in?" he asked. "How could they let you go?"

"It's my turn, I think," she said with a grin.

"Answer me first," he demanded.

She almost jumped when he touched the hand she had resting on the table.

"It was an Italian restaurant. And yes, I loved it. But I needed a change." What an understatement. She'd needed an entire life make-over.

She turned her hand upside down and let his fingers rest on her palm.

They were holding hands—sort of.

"This *is* quite a change out here. I went to Chicago on a school FFA trip years and years ago, and I liked it, even though it was a bit overwhelming with the noise and the people."

"FFA?" she asked.

"Future Farmers of America," he answered.

"Ah! My high school didn't have that, I don't think." She frowned. The Catholic school had many different groups but nothing about farming.

"Naw, it's a farm kid thing." He shrugged. "Each year they hold a national convention somewhere, and one year it was in Chicago. So, I'm wondering: how you are coping with the huge difference?"

"Doesn't have to be a big difference." She shrugged. "I can keep cooking my Italian out here, can't I? Maybe not for as many people, but I can still do what I love."

"You could cook nothing but Italian for the rest of my life and I'd be happy." He smiled and paused.

She wondered if he was telling her in his own way that she had won the competition. Phyllis was as good as Laura was, even more well-rounded in meal prep. "Well, that and your biscuits and gravy."

She laughed. "I'll see what I can do." She stared at him long and hard, studying the light whisker growth on his face, the rough angles of his nose that looked like it had been broken more than once. She wondered if the tan on his face reached the rest of his body. He had worn long-sleeved shirts every day since she met him.

"My first question is simple. Did you sleep with Angel or in any way have a sexual relationship?"

"That's two questions, I think." He squeezed her hand and smiled. "You sure don't pull any punches, do you?" He laughed. "No and no. She came on to me, not vice versa. She's a pretty girl, but I'm her boss—make that I *was* her boss, and I would not cross that line."

Well, where did that leave Laura then? She wanted to ask, but he was faster.

"Have you ever been married?" he asked, pulling his hand away to break another gooey, chocolate chip cookie in half.

"No." She shook her head. "Not even close." She pushed her hair out of her eyes. "Where is Connor's mom?"

"Last I heard," he said around a mouthful of cookie, "she was in Amarillo. She follows the rodeo circuit. Has a thing for cowboys and horses."

"Is that how you met her?"

"You're cheating again," he said, pointing at her. "Where are your parents?"

Here they come, she thought. The stuff she didn't want to talk about, the details of her life she had changed to be safe.

"My father passed away recently." *True.* "That's what really made me want to leave Chicago. I realized how short life is." And how short my life could have been. "My mother is grieving as only she would know how. She's in Florida with her friends." Well, Mama Vita was in Florida, not visiting friends but maybe, hopefully making a few.

"I'm sorry for your loss, Laura."

She looked away. If he only knew just how much she had lost.

Time slipped on as they sat quietly. She had so many questions about him, personal ones that were probably inappropriate to ask her boss. Finally, she tapped his foot under the table and caught his attention.

"Did you marry Connor's mom?" Laura asked quietly. She really was getting personal here, felt uncomfortable asking, but, well....

"No," he answered simply, failing to elaborate. "Do you have siblings?"

"Yes. A brother and a sister." She omitted the fact she was a twin. If he happened to check the obituary section of the *Chicago Trib*, it clearly read that she and Vinny were twins. Caleb would never find a Marshall in that paper, though, which might lead to more uncomfortable questions in the future.

"How did you meet Connor's mom?"

"Her name is Christie." He wiped his mouth with a napkin and took her hand again, this time twining his fingers through hers. "I was riding bulls for the hell of it back then, just doing local rodeos." He took a sip of milk. "Burwell, a town not too far from here, has a pretty big shindig every summer, and I was there. And so was she. We spent most of the summer together and when August came, rather than moving on, she moved in here with me."

Laura nodded, digesting the facts along with the cookies.

"Where are your brother and sister?"

That was a good question. And she had to recall what their new names were when she answered. This was tougher than it should be.

"Mike is in North Carolina. Liz is in Alaska." At least she got that much right. "Why did you become a rancher?"

"Why did you become a cook?" He shot back.

He laughed, and so did she.

"It was in my blood," she answered. "My great grandma lived with me until I was fifteen." She took another cookie. "She was old when she died, just shy of one hundred. She didn't speak very good English, so she taught me Italian and how to cook and bake. I knew what I wanted to do from the time I was a child."

"I could say the same." He rubbed the back of her hand with his thumb. "My grandfather ranched this land; Dad did, too. I knew I had to carry it forward, especially after Connor was born, 'cause I had to carry on his legacy. Now with Holly pregnant, Josh and I will have to look harder at expanding even further."

She nodded. She also knew he and Josh didn't own the place outright. Someone else had stepped in at some point to help them with the financials. "So, Hank gave up on it then?"

"Hank was never involved," he ground out.

"But I thought you just said—"

"Hank is my *stepdad*," Caleb answered before she even finished her thought.

"Sorry." She frowned. "I misunderstood."

"You'll meet him tomorrow," he said.

The sound of gravel crunching under a heavy load could be heard outside the open window. A deep, loud horn sounded.

Caleb stood up. "Finally."

She sniffed. "Sorry I wasn't more entertaining."

"I didn't mean it that way, Laura."

He bent forward and kissed her cheek, just in front of her ear. She turned her face the required few inches to get his lips to rest upon hers. The kiss started slowly and softly, but soon he was parting her lips and twining her tongue with his.

His hands found the sides of her face and held her until a rap at the door pulled them apart.

"Gotta go," he said quietly, his voice thick. He rubbed his thumb across her lips, caressing the area he'd just kissed, and then walked out the door to meet the driver.

"That was nice," she whispered and then giggled. She had gotten her answers and a kiss, to boot. Feeling like a giddy teenager, she turned her attention back to the computer, happy she had been able to set up the secret accounts with her family before they all went into hiding, enabling her to still stay in contact, albeit from a great distance.

"Bryan found the tank." Josh caught Caleb just as he was leaving the office for the evening. "It's empty, but the registration number matches ours."

"Where was it?"

"In a damn ditch." Josh chuckled. "Bryan was driving through Fowler's place and saw it."

"What was Bryan doing out there? Busting people for making out?"

"I think he was the one screwing some chick."

Caleb laughed. "He's got so many women, don't know how he keeps them all straight."

"Jealous?"

"Not so much today, no. It would take an awful lot to knock me out of my good mood." Caleb sat at his desk. "We got a hell of a price for the grain."

"Is it enough to get us out of the red? Can we finally be done with Don and his stupid ideas?"

"That's what I'm hoping," Caleb answered.

"Hot damn." Josh clapped. "It'll be nice when the place is running at full capacity under *our* management, not his."

Caleb just nodded; he'd thought the same thing for quite a while. Josh left his coat on and replaced the hat he'd earlier thrown on his desk.

"You and Holly want to go to the cattlemen's meeting?"

"Naw." Josh shook his head. "She's so sick in the mornings. We'll just keep an eye on things here." Josh crossed his arms. "We'll save some money that way. I've got to get better at setting something aside for diapers." He laughed and opened the door to leave. "Oh, damn! I forgot to tell you. We found a couple cows down today. It looks isolated, but I'm hauling them into the vet just to be sure."

Caleb couldn't imagine the missing fertilizer tank and the cow deaths were related. How could they be? "I don't have a good feeling about this." He tended to be the more cautious of the two of them.

"I have to jet. We'll just have to keep a closer eye on the place." Josh slapped Caleb's shoulder and grabbed for the doorknob. "Holly wants to go to North Platte tonight. You going out with everyone?"

"Nope." Caleb leaned back in his chair, entwining his fingers behind his head. "I'm going to finish the paperwork and then hit the hay."

"Sounds boring to me. I'll see ya in the morning." Josh left the office, banging the heavy steel door closed on his way out.

Boring, maybe, but Caleb didn't want to leave the ranch tonight. If one cow died it wouldn't be so strange, but to have two go down? The missing tank was still eating at his gut. Hopefully they weren't related, but with harvest it was a damn awful time to have unexpected things pop up.

Wrapped in a warm, handmade quilt she'd brought down with her from her room, Laura was curled up on the screened-in porch at the front of the house. It had been too many years since she'd slowed down enough to enjoy a sunset. Especially on a Saturday night. Adjusting to the isolation of the Sandhills was going far better than she'd expected when she applied for the job.

The men were a loud bunch tonight, getting stoked for their evening in town. Phyllis was excited too, virtually bubbling the whole time she made supper. Laura had fixed Phyllis's hair again and helped her with makeup. She was wearing another one of Laura's outfits, thinking her new look was lucky. She had met "someone special"—that was all she would tell Laura about the guy—and she was seeing him again tonight. They were going bowling, one of the few diversions the town offered.

Laura hadn't seen Caleb since their private interlude in the kitchen just before the driver arrived to pick up the grain. Her senses had been tingling all day—reeling, really— from the contact she'd had with him, and she found herself smiling from time to time, remembering his kiss.

What in heaven's name was she doing? She couldn't let herself get involved with the man—or any man—at the moment. It was far too soon. What if the gangster pricks were still after her? She had no past, could never tell Caleb who she *really* was. Besides, if she did tell him, chances are he wouldn't want her anyway. What guy would want to be linked to a mob family?

The hot chocolate tasted good, and with the wind gently blowing on her, she felt calmer, more relaxed than she could remember. She waved and called goodbye to the guys as they loaded up and headed back to the trailer houses to get ready for their night in town.

Phyllis came bursting out the door. When she saw Laura, she stopped. "Sure you don't want to come? The guys would wait for you to get ready."

"No. You go on ahead." Laura waved her off. The idea of bowling or sitting in a bar wasn't as appealing as drinking hot chocolate and eventually closing her eyes on this screened-in porch, wrapped in the security of the vintage tattered and battered quilt, just feeling the wind gently brush her face…. "Have a great time, and good luck with your date!"

"Thanks." Phyllis giggled and ran off to the pickup waiting for her.

Laura couldn't believe how quickly the woman had come out of her shell.

What was Caleb doing tonight? Were he and Conner hanging out, or had he found a different babysitter for tonight? She tried to tell herself the kiss that afternoon hadn't really mattered. But it did.

She leaned back in the comfortable chair and closed her eyes as she heard the last two pickups pull out of the drive. The chair seemed to get even more comfortable when she shifted, and soon she gave in to the relaxation of the breeze and comfort of the blanket and found sleep.

Like a moth, Caleb was drawn to the low light burning on the screened-in porch. He'd figured Laura had trailed off to town with Phyllis, but he'd been wrong. Here she was, as quiet as a mouse, sleeping. He chuckled and sat on an empty chair to watch her. He didn't want to wake her; he'd done that enough already.

Caleb had gotten off the phone with Jasper a short time ago. He'd called to remind Caleb about the convention in the coming week. Jasper was planning to invite Phyllis to go with him, provided Caleb didn't need her. Like his mom, Jasper too, had heard about problems out here, knew they were down to two cooks.

"How long have you been out here?" Laura stretched and glanced at the gold watch on her wrist.

"Oh, just a little bit." He smiled back.

"It's dark." She laughed and sat up straighter. "I guess I was tired."

"Everyone's gone already. Hope you didn't want to go to town tonight."

"Nope. I'm enjoying being lazy." She stretched again and pushed the quilt off her shoulders. "What a beautiful night."

"It feels like fall."

"You don't like fall?" She grabbed her forgotten cup, took a drink, and made a face. She caught him looking at her and grimaced. "Cold chocolate. Ick." She stood up. "Would you like something? Coffee, maybe?"

"I'm fine. And to answer your question, I love fall. I think it's my favorite season. We don't have the trees you have in Illinois, but the few we do have look pretty this time of year."

She walked by him with her cup, and he grabbed her free hand. "Will you come back out?"

"Sure." She nodded and squeezed his hand.

The wall between the kitchen and the porch muffled the sounds. He could hear running water and then the microwave door shutting. He'd enjoyed learning something about her that afternoon. Would she be up for more questions tonight?

His heart was feeling *something* for her. The purely male part of him had an immediate reaction that first night. Amazing, really, seeing as she wasn't his type. He thought maybe he was just so desperate for a woman that anyone would do, but after the confrontation with Angel and the evening with Jenny, he'd realized that wasn't the case.

After the trucker left with the grain in the afternoon, he'd run the budget numbers, using a couple of scenarios, and worked it so he could hire both Laura and Phyllis. They got along well—probably wouldn't be bosom buddie—but at least they could share the labor. He hoped Laura would consider taking care of Connor as part of her responsibilities; maybe then his mother wouldn't have to drive out here so often.

"I'm baaaack." She grinned and plopped down back where she'd been sitting.

"I'm glad." He rested his ankle on his opposite knee and folded his hands in his lap. "I've got more questions for you."

"You do?" She took a sip from her mug. "Okay." She put the mug down and rubbed her hands on her thigh then clapped. "Bring 'em on."

He chuckled. "What do you think about the ranch so far?"

"Hmm…. Here I expected something deep." She crossed her legs and leaned back in the chair, covering herself with the blanket.

"It's quiet, desolate. But I like your men and your family." She grabbed her mug and took a sip. "The kitchen is terrific and having free rein is fun. So, all in all, I like it."

"What about your family?"

"What about them?" She shoved her legs underneath her and sat in a position his son would call "crisscross apple sauce."

"Well, you're so far from all them. Don't you miss them?"

"Sure." She shrugged. "But we are so spread out. None of them are living where I would want to, so I guess email and texting is the best way to stay in touch." She took a sip from her mug. "What other questions have you got for me?"

"Would you like to stay here?" He blurted it out, uncertain how to phrase it.

"Really? You've decided already?" Skepticism laced her voice.

"I think I'd like to keep both you and Phyllis on if you want. There would be one more job I'd add in for you, though."

"Please don't tell me the cow inventory thing." She laughed.

He loved her laugh. It was so genuine.

"I don't think I could do that again," she added.

"No deal then." He stood, amused by her face as he pretended to leave and then sat back down. "That was a way for you to see what goes on, on the ranch. There's a lot more to it, of course, but you got just a taste."

"Good." She stretched her legs out in front of her and crossed her ankles. "So, what would these tasks be?"

"I'd let you do all the ordering. I imagine you'll know better what we need for the kitchen and house. Like I told you, I did it for Stella because of the language problem."

"That would be fine," she agreed. "Once I get the hang of it, I can come up with menus ahead of time."

He chuckled. "Organized, aren't you?"

"I'm not a big one for surprises, so the better prepared I am, the better I feel."

He studied her, holding back the urge to pull her over onto his lap and kiss the life out of her, to use his body to make her warm, instead of the tattered blanket she was clinging to.

"I'm not very spontaneous myself. That's why this whole idea for holding a contest to find a new cook threw me for a loop."

"Are you mad you let Josh talk you into it?"

"How did you know?"

She chuckled. "Your mom."

"Figures." He shook his head and leaned forward, his elbows resting on his knees.

"What would you think about adding Connor to your list of responsibilities?"

"Babysitting?" She shrugged and pulled back slightly. "Never been around kids. But, sure, I can give it a try."

She nodded, and he felt as if the whole world had lifted off his shoulders.

"Drive him to school, get him ready, that kind of thing?" she asked.

"Exactly," he agreed. "Con will be thrilled. He sings your praises from dawn to dark." He leaned back in the chair again.

"I think he's pretty special too." She took a sip from her mug. "Does Christie have any contact with him?"

"No." It hurt to admit it, even after all this time. "She wrote us off pretty quickly after Conner was born. Stayed on about a year and then got the wanderlust and was gone."

"Do you still have a thing for her?"

How to answer that one? He didn't miss Christie, but it was a shame that their son would never know his mother, never have the love of his mother. "Let me put it this way. If she had stayed, I would still be with her. But I'm not pining away for her. I quit that a long time ago."

"Jenny?"

"That's just a casual thing with her."

"What? The sex or the relationship?" she quipped.

He burst into laughter, shocked. "You're sassy tonight. You must have been tired this afternoon, huh? Your questions were rather tame then."

"Tame or lame?" She laughed. "I'm just feeling uninhibited tonight."

Did she feel more comfortable with him?

"Well, you know, two can play this game." He rubbed his hands together and smiled. "How about a silly game of truth or dare?"

"No fun with only two people."

"Oh, we could probably make it interesting."

He saw her hesitate. Did she worry there might be a question she would not want to answer or a task she was unwilling to complete?

"Fine," she said.

"Ladies first this time. Truth or dare?"

"Dare."

That surprised him, as did her bright smile.

"Tonight, we're not boss and employee, got it?" Was that his voice? It sounded seductive…and thick.

"What are we then?"

He shrugged. "Just two people getting to know each other."

"Agreed."

She raised a brow in an unspoken challenge for him to come up with something creative.

"I dare you, Miss Laura, to kiss me like you've never kissed a man before."

Laura's heart rate doubled and she found it hard to breathe. She forced herself to relax, play it cool, but it was difficult. "Hmm, that's quite a challenge, Mr. Caleb. Should I accept?"

"You don't have a choice. If you don't accept it, I get to give out consequences."

"Sounds interesting, maybe I should refuse just to see what you'd do to me." She stared at him, trying her best to look seductive and then felt foolish and walked over to him.

He sat still, his hands on his knees, watching her in silence. She snuggled onto his lap and kissed his forehead.

She was done, and she wondered how long it would take for him to realize it.

"That's it?"

She shrugged. "I have never kissed a man's forehead before."

He laughed and wrapped his arms around her waist, pulling her closer. She knew he'd been expecting more, but she wouldn't relent. Not yet, anyway. He smelled so manly, a combination of the outdoors and leather. The muscles under his heavy work shirt contracted as she wrapped an arm around his shoulder.

"Truth or dare?" She whispered the question in his ear.

"Truth, I suppose?"

"Did you love Christie?"

"That's an easy one. You came up with it so quickly, you must have had that one burning in your brain." He leaned against the back of the chair, looking deep into her eyes. "No. I tried to show her respect because she was the mother of my child, but that was it. She was pretty too. Funny." He chuckled, as if remembering some private joke. "But I didn't really love her. If I did, I wouldn't have let her go."

Laura nodded, liking the honesty, wishing she too, could reveal as much about herself to him.

"How about another dare?" he teased.

"Truth this time, I think." She took a deep breath and then exhaled.

"Are you wanted by the law?"

She burst into laughter, relieved she could be honest. "No."

"It's not that funny." He sighed, an offended look on his scrunched face.

"I'm a cook, not a criminal."

He touched her hair—caressed it really—and then moved his hand to her cheek. "It's just inconceivable to me that a woman as pretty and cultured as you are would leave Chicago and come out here to the middle of nowhere to cook for a bunch of men."

"You think I'm pretty?" She grinned. He'd given her a compliment and probably didn't even realize it.

He cupped the back of her head and pulled her face toward him, touching his lips to hers. The kiss threw sparks in the air. It must have. Laura had no concept of the outside world as she snaked her arm around Caleb's neck. Just when she thought he'd pull back, he surprised her by deepening the kiss, teasing her tongue with his.

His hand left her hair and trailed down her back to just above her waist, where he let it stay. She was the one to pull away, feeling lightheaded and a bit dazed.

"That was nice," she said. *The understatement of the year.*

"Using me for practice, are ya?"

"Dad?" Connor broke their intimate moment. "Dad?" The call got louder as the little boy neared.

"Sorry," Caleb said quietly to Laura, before calling out, "On the porch, Con."

Laura hopped off Caleb's lap and sat back on her chair, feeling embarrassed like she had the time she'd been busted by Pop while making out with her high school boyfriend on the living room couch.

She'd never dated a man with a child. But then again, were they really dating?

Laura shut her bedroom door early the next morning, ready to go for her jog and get the day underway. She was excited to see Caleb again, disappointed their time had been cut short last night. Connor was such a sweet boy, Laura could hardly complain about sharing Caleb with his son.

"What the…Phyllis, are you just getting home?" Laura stopped short halfway down the stairs as Phyllis appeared at the bottom.

The woman was still wearing her clothes from the night before, most of the makeup had disappeared, and her hair—well, it looked a little like bedhead.

"Jasper and I, um, got pretty friendly last night." She flushed scarlet and met Laura on the stairs. "You should see his house! My word, it's a huge mansion, and the poor man lives all alone. Well, there's Sebastian, his dog, but no one else. Can you believe it?"

At a loss for words, Laura let Phyllis babble on.

"We get along so well. He's a couple years older than me, and he's really good friends with Caleb; in fact, that's how we met—at the bar—with Caleb. He's handsome and rich, and I think he likes me a lot." She stopped to take a breath. "He asked if I would go to a conference with him next weekend!"

"Did you say yes?" Laura asked, thinking the answer was obvious.

"I said I would if it was okay with Caleb. Do you know what he said then?"

Laura shook her head; she had no idea.

"He said, 'I already asked him!' Can you believe it?" She tugged harder on Laura's sleeve. "He called to get Caleb's okay before he asked. So thoughtful."

"And to think when I first met you, I thought you'd be as quiet as a mouse." Laura laughed. "Go take a shower, and I'll meet you downstairs for a cup of coffee."

"Oh, breakfast!" Phyllis smacked herself in the forehead. "I forgot."

"I've got it covered." Laura pointed Phyllis toward her room and jogged down the remaining stairs.

She went into the kitchen to get the coffee going, not expecting anyone else to be up this early.

"Good morning! My, oh my, Connor, you're up early!" Laura grinned. "Did you make the coffee for me?" she joked.

"No, silly." He looked up briefly from the handheld game he was playing. "I can't make that stuff. Dad did. Miss Laura, can I have some more milk?"

Laura reached for it just as Caleb entered the kitchen.

"I'll get it," he said.

She met his gaze with a big smile. He was all seriousness today, wearing his usual denim shirt and jeans. He had shaved off his whiskers from the night before and looked good enough to kiss, which she very much was tempted to do.

He poured his son more milk and winked at her, before heading to the coffee pot to pour himself some caffeine energy. He filled a mug for her, brought it to the table, and sat across from her, next to Connor.

"I meant to ask you something last night."

"More questions, Caleb?" She chuckled.

"Funny girl." He touched her foot under the table with his boot. "I wanted to know if you would go with me to the cattlemen's conference next weekend?"

"Oh, the one Phyllis and Jasper are going to?"

"How did you know?" A look of surprise scattered across his face.

"I saw her upstairs as I was coming down."

"So, she made it home, huh?" He smiled. "Yes, that same conference. We'd stay Thursday and Friday night. There's a fancy banquet-slash-dance thing on Friday with awards." He paused. "You'd have your own room, of course."

"Who will take care of me?" Connor asked quietly, looking at his dad with big, sad puppy eyes.

"Grandma, of course," Caleb told his son. He turned to Laura. "Ma will cook for the farmhands on those days too."

"In that case, I'd love to." Laura's heart pounded at the idea of spending some one-on-one time with Caleb and really getting to know him.

Getting off the ranch, back into the public, would be a challenge. She had a feeling she would be constantly looking over her shoulder, but what was the chance anyone would know her at a cattlemen's conference?

CHAPTER
TEN

THE DAYS WERE SO PACKED with work, she seemed to fly through them, only realizing as she fell into bed at night just how much she had done in a day. Laura and Phyllis got along well, they shared the chores, each doing what they enjoyed most, and it seemed to be working out just fine for everyone.

Caleb had been even busier, tying up loose ends before the trip so he could relax and enjoy the reprieve from the ranch for a few days while they were gone. Laura didn't see him much—usually only for a short bit in the evening before he went back out to the office to get paperwork and payroll done.

Today, she had worked with Mary Grace to get their schedule straight. In a few hours, she and Caleb would be headed to Wyoming for the conference with Jasper, whom Laura had still not met, and Phyllis.

Laura wasn't so worried about the goons from Chicago anymore. She felt safe here on the ranch, knew if she stayed near Caleb at the conference and surrounded herself with other people, she would be fine. But she was still troubled about her heart, fearful she might lose it completely to Caleb, a serious man who valued his freedom and enjoyed the solitary isolation of his

Nebraska ranch. He was a man who didn't seem to need a woman, except as a housekeeper and to help raise his son.

And she *was* losing her heart. Caleb tugged at her heartstrings every time he ruffled his son's hair. When he'd touched her hand under the table the day before, she'd melted, and when he kissed her, she just about fell to pieces.

She had been alone for three years, maybe four. She could hardly recall her last date, just knew it happened soon after Bella Vita began to succeed. Men were interested, she knew, but intimidated by her reputation, poorly earned, as an ice princess. She was a businesswoman, driven by the desire to make Bella Vita the best restaurant on or near Michigan Avenue in the heart of Chicago. She'd done it, met her goals, had finally made a profit, and then she'd been forced to abandon it.

She was looking forward to the new challenges at the ranch, perhaps not as difficult or taxing as planning a dinner party for hundreds as she had at Bella Vita. This would be her life now: planning meals for twenty men, keeping a house organized, and caring for an adorable, little boy. Simpler but, hopefully, just as fulfilling.

Could she allow herself to fall for Caleb? The FBI guy never told her not to get involved with anyone—just to be cautious and not tell anyone about her past. She'd been honest with Caleb to this point, although deliberately vague.

She wanted to know what Caleb expected from her the next few days. Was she just a one-off like Jenny had been or was he playing for higher, more permanent stakes? And which would Laura prefer, if given the choice? Torn between the two options, she wasn't sure which way she was leaning. She wanted him, felt desire for him clear to her core every time he was around, but was it too soon?

Laura looked up at the clock again, bored, drumming her fingers on the kitchen table, waiting for Caleb to come in from the office. She just wanted the cards laid out on the table so she would know what to expect. She hated surprises, and it wasn't too much to ask for, to have him voice his intentions. At least, she didn't think it was.

She packed light, knowing she would have to hit a department store or two when they reached Casper. She'd left all her pretty, fancy dresses behind, locked away in a metal storage shed in a ritzy Chicago suburb, where she was convinced her belongings would be safe. Caleb said the dinner was fancy; he was wearing a suit and a tie. She'd brought nothing that would remotely be suitable. She included her running gear, planning to keep up a bit with her routine, even in a hotel.

That was the next concern. The hotel. So far, they'd only kissed, nothing more, so he shouldn't expect they'd have sex, right? Should she ask? She shook her head, angry she was obsessing about things that weren't relevant at the moment.

She glanced at the clock on the wall yet again, wondered if the battery had died, as the hands seemed to have frozen. Why was she waiting for him? She stood, determined to go out to the office and get his butt moving. Mary Grace had been out to the ranch for Connor and had left over an hour ago. Laura was ready to leave too, and afraid if she had to wait much longer, she might chicken out—give in to her concern about going out in public—and stay home.

She pulled the phone from the hook and dialed the office number, which was posted next to the receiver on the wall. After four rings, voicemail picked up. She decided not to leave a message. Antsy and impatient, she snagged the truck keys off the nail by the back door, went through the breezeway and into the garage, where she found the extra truck parked. Climbing up into the cab, she fired the engine and pulled the truck out of the garage.

Two minutes later, she pulled up next to Caleb's extended-cab pickup. Noting the light on inside the office portion of the building, she put the truck into park, cut the engine, and climbed out. She opened the heavy steel door to the building and followed the sound of twangy country music, hoping the sound would lead her to him. She rapped on the door of the office and went in when he told her to.

"What's up?" she asked him with a smile.

Several short stacks of paperwork surrounded him at the desk. And although he looked up at her briefly, she got the immediate feeling there was a problem. Or she wasn't welcome in the office.

"Is there something I can help with?" Laura walked closer and rested her hip against his desk. "Anything?"

"You anxious to get going?" He didn't look up from the spreadsheet in front of him, marking with pencil as he studied the numbers.

"I…." What could she say? "Yes, I guess I am."

"What do you know about budgets?" In one fluid motion, he flung his pencil on top of the papers, sat against the back of his seat, and looked up at her.

"Enough," she said. "Where's the problem?"

"I was hoping we would finally be in the black after this harvest." He glanced back at the paper.

"And you're not?"

"Nope. Not yet." He shoved a hand through his hair. "I'll have to get financing for another year."

"What about your plans for the guest portion of the house?"

He'd mentioned having guests in the near future, that she and Phyllis would have more duties when people started coming to stay.

"We'll start in the spring. Start advertising after the first of the year. I've got all those costs figured in." He stared at her and then held out a hand. "Come here, would you?"

She took his hand and let him pull her toward him, quickly getting comfortable on his lap.

"I needed a distraction," he said. "How did you know?"

"Must be my psychic abilities." She laughed, wrapping an arm around his shoulder and initiating a kiss.

His hand found the side of her breast and stayed still only a mere second before his thumb began to tease her nipple through her shirt and bra. The pressure made her wiggle on his lap, quick, hot desire soaring through her body.

She reached for the buttons of his rough denim shirt and slowly slipped them open. She wanted to feel his chest, knew she would feel hard muscles. He caught her hand before she succeeded and like a wet blanket, drew her back to the present, feeling hot and more than a little bothered.

"Whoa." She exhaled.

"Whoa, is right." He lifted her hand to his lips. "You're beautiful." He dropped her hand and caressed her cheek. "Passionate. I could lose my head pretty quickly with you."

"Is that a problem?"

He laughed and pushed her off his lap. "It damn well could be, lady." He clicked the desk lamp off. "I doubt my mind could focus on numbers like it should, so we might just as well head out. You go on ahead; I'll be right behind you."

Damn, he was hard. Too hard to even stand up without it being obvious. Glad she hadn't argued when he'd told her to go ahead, he finally stood to turn off the computers and set the answering machine to pick up on the first ring.

She was a hot little thing, lit him up like a match. He'd wanted nothing more than to take her, then and there right on his desk. Screw the budget. He hadn't felt his body come alive that fast ever, or not in years anyway.

She was so soft. Her breasts just fit in his hand and….

Why was he thinking like that? It was making the agony worse.

The next few days would prove to be interesting. Maybe if they did it, just once, he'd get the sex out of his system, and they'd be able to move on. Laura didn't seem like the clingy type.

Who was he kidding?

She was the type of gal he'd never be able to let go. She was like a potato chip— once would never be enough.

If only he knew what she was hiding from him. Their conversations only went so far before she backed away into the shell she had created around herself. Maybe in time, she'd let him in. Maybe even sometime over the next few days when they were alone together, just the two of them, he'd get an insight into her secrets.

Caleb shut and locked the door to the building as he left, still concerned about the odd activity on the ranch. That morning, the vet had verified the dead cows Josh had found had been poisoned. Each had enough rat poison in their systems to wipe out five cows. To make matters even worse, three were cows missing and a fourth one had been found slaughtered—and not by a wild animal.

Bryan, the sheriff, said it looked like a strange ritual killing of some sort. This wasn't the first time some sick bastard had come out to steal one of Caleb's cows to use as a sacrifice for a pagan ritual. In fact, this was about the third such instance. The first time, he'd been freaked out; now, not so much. Being October, with Halloween coming, people had to expect that unusual things would start happening. But the poisoning made no sense.

Caleb drove the short distance home, glad he had packed his clothes that morning before heading out to work. Laura was excited to get going, and that made him happy, glad she wanted to be with him. He might need to put a few miles behind him before he would begin to unwind and forget about the crap happening at the Morning Glory, but Caleb believed Laura would have the skills to help him let it all go.

"Dang it!" Laura broke a freshly manicured nail as the zipper on her suitcase stuck. She gnawed off the remainder of the nail, wishing she hadn't spent so much time on the foolish feminine primping.

She lifted the now-sealed bag off the bed and pulled it into the hallway and then down the staircase. Phyllis was waiting for her in the main room, looking at a *People* magazine.

"Hey."

"Are you ready for the trip?" Phyllis asked.

"I think so. I need to stop at a store and get a dress for the dance, but otherwise, yep, I should be."

"Did Caleb tell you he wants to keep us both as employees?" Phyllis asked her.

"Yeah." Laura nodded and sat down across from Phyllis. "I think it's a pretty good idea."

"Sure you want to take care of Connor?" Phyllis set aside the magazine and crossed her legs.

"I like him," Laura said. "A lot. It should be fine. I guess it will mean more housework for you, though."

"Well, as I was expecting to do it all, splitting stuff with you should be just fine," Phyllis said. "Less work, same pay. I'd say that's a win-win."

"Having another woman around to chat with will make it easier to live out here too," Laura said.

"What's going on with you and Caleb?" Phyllis whispered.

"I'm not sure." Laura looked away, embarrassed to think about the man. She wasn't ready to say what she thought was going on. She didn't want to start something with Caleb she couldn't finish.

"You like him?"

"Yeah," Laura admitted. "He's handsome and nice. Maybe a bit gruff, but I think that comes from being around men all day."

"He's got a nice smile." Phyllis turned on the couch to lay down.

"I like his chin." Laura laughed, meeting Phyllis's eyes. "And his walk. Those bowed legs are kinda sexy."

"That's an understatement." Phyllis giggled. "Jasper is pretty handsome, but he's older, got grays running through his hair. He's a happy guy. I think you'll like him."

"I'm sure." Laura nodded. "If he and Caleb are friends, he must be a decent guy."

"Will you share a room with him, ya think?" Phyllis' eyes were shut.

"I don't think so, no." Laura shook her head, trying not to think about what had happened earlier in the office.

"I suppose we'll share a room," Phyllis said. "We've already slept together, so it's not too much of a leap. I wonder if there's a fancy lingerie shop in Casper."

Laura laughed. That was the last thing she would have thought of. "I'll bet in a city that size, there would be somewhere to shop for that type of thing."

"All set, ladies?" Caleb called in from the kitchen. "I'll meet you out at the truck."

She and Phyllis exchanged glances, and Laura wondered if Phyllis was nearly as excited as she was. Her heart was pounding hard, threatening to leap from her chest, and she knew if she looked in a mirror, her face would be flushed. They left the house and headed toward Caleb's pickup and waited to see where he wanted them to stow their bags.

"You're lucky, Laura." Phyllis shook her head. "I don't know if you can see the looks that guy gives you." She hooked her thumb over her shoulder. "But I think he's in love."

"Probably just lust." Laura smiled.

Caleb joined them, his bowed-legged swagger making her crazy. That, and the cleft in his square chin. And his lips…and, well, other things….

"All set?" Caleb opened the passenger door, hung his suit bag on a hook in the back of the cab, and then loaded their suitcases into the bed of the truck, pulling the liner shut. He helped Phyllis crawl up into the back seat and then with a gentle hand on her rear, he eased Laura into the passenger seat. She looked back to see if he meant it as a grope and was rewarded with a sly wink.

She shook her head, reminding herself it was what it was….Just lust.

"Jasper lives about a half hour from here." Caleb climbed in behind the wheel. "He's got a nice spread doesn't he, Phyllis?"

"Spread?" Phyllis squeaked.

Caleb laughed and glanced at Laura, but she didn't quite know what to make of the question, either.

"Nice land, house, buildings. Spread is a nickname for a ranch," Caleb explained.

"Oh." Phyllis chuckled. "Yes, he does. And a big truck."

Caleb laughed again. "It's a duallie," he explained to Laura. "Four wheels in the back instead of two."

"Yeah, that's what he called it," Phyllis answered. "It's loud inside, a lot louder than your truck."

The conversation trailed off there. It was starting to get dark, a beautiful sunset made up of pretty lines of pinks and mauves leading their way. Although the sky was calm, her heart was racing with the excitement of it all. Laura got lost in her thoughts, wondering what the upcoming days would bring. What if he wanted her to sleep with him?

"Have you ever been this far west, Laura?" Caleb asked her.

"Sure." Laura turned toward him. "I've been skiing in Colorado and Utah. Been to Vegas and LA I went to Seattle once. Phoenix too."

"Really? Man, somehow I pictured you confined to the Midwest."

She laughed. "They did let me leave home every now and again for good behavior."

Caleb and Phyllis laughed.

Thinking about those trips, mostly spent with her family, caused a sudden pang of loneliness. Going from a family of five to a singular existence was damn hard.

What was Mama Vita doing right now? Had she made friends in Florida yet? The FBI had helped her get set up in a penthouse overlooking the ocean. She loved the water and had to be in heaven. Mama didn't like being alone, would certainly remarry. It hurt like the devil to think Laura could never hug her mother again and Mama wouldn't be able to attend her children's weddings or meet any of her grandchildren.

Laura had to get her mind on better things or she'd start bawling like a baby. She switched her thoughts to Barrow, Alaska, to what her sister Maria called the tip of the world, where she was squirreled away, teaching at a high school. And then poor Vinny, Laura's twin, living large in a cabin on a beach on North Carolina's Outer Banks. He'd gotten the good deal. Laura wasn't sure why the FBI thought Maria would be happy in Alaska or why they'd stuck Laura on a cattle ranch, but surely they'd had their reasons. She was thankful the FBI had helped them at all, given the fact they refused to be fully integrated into the protection program.

Maria's last email said Garbaldo had found Vinny. Laura wasn't sure what that meant, other than it was in her best interest to watch her back. Vinny hadn't testified against Garbaldo; instead, he'd just disappeared one day.

Caleb took her hand and squeezed it. "Your face is certainly expressive. One minute I thought you were about to cry, and now you seem to be laughing at something."

"Just thinking." She shrugged with a smile.

"I'm glad you came with me," he said softly, meeting her eyes. "I haven't taken anyone with me in years. Jasper is the same." He glanced into the back seat at Phyllis.

"I like him, Caleb. He says you are one of the best friends he's got."

"I'd agree with that; he's an all-around good guy." Caleb nodded and raised this hand to point at the top of the hill. "That's his place."

Laura was in awe of what she saw. The house, lit up like a Christmas tree, perched on top of the ridge, overlooking a deep valley. "The view must be awesome!"

"It is," Phyllis and Caleb answered in unison, and then both chuckled.

They pulled up to the house and Caleb climbed out. Jasper was waiting at the door for them. Laura watched as he and Caleb kenneled Jasper's pretty yellow Labradors.

She turned back to Phyllis. "You want to cuddle with him, or should I scoot in back?"

"Come on in back. We'll whisper about things and make them think we're talking about them." She laughed.

Laura opened the door and climbed out, then got into the back seat with Phyllis. "This is fun. I haven't been on a double date in years. Well, really I haven't been on a *date* in years."

"You're kidding me?"

Laura got cozy in the spot next to Phyllis. "No." Laura shook her head. "Why are you so surprised?"

"Have you looked in a mirror lately?"

Laura rolled her eyes.

"I'm serious. I would kill to have looks like you."

"Phyllis, you are—"

"Don't say it." Phyllis cut Laura short. "Because it's not true. You helped me, by letting me borrow your clothes and by fixing my makeup and hair. You've helped me look better, but I am still not even remotely pretty."

"Well, here comes one guy I bet would disagree with that."

Caleb and Jasper walked to the pickup, joking about something, and then they split, Caleb stashing Jasper's suitcase in the back and then climbing in behind the wheel, Jasper sitting in the front passenger seat.

"Hi ya, Phyllis." He reached over into the back seat and squeezed her hand. "You must be Laura." He smiled and shook her hand.

Caleb put the truck into gear. Jasper turned back long enough to put on his seatbelt and then sat sideways in the seat to see Phyllis and Laura.

They talked briefly, but soon, the only sounds were the murmurs of Jasper and Caleb, who were talking in the darkness of the cab, and the monotonous roar of the tires on the highway. Laura drifted off to sleep, catching sight of the lights of Ainsworth just before dozing off.

CHAPTER
ELEVEN

"So, what's on your mind?" Caleb asked Jasper as they pulled out of the gas station in Lusk, just over the Wyoming border.

Jasper was driving now, having taken a quick nap like the two women in the back seat. "I'm thinking marriage."

"Seriously?" Caleb couldn't believe it. He knew Jasper had it bad, but he'd only known Phyllis a short time.

"Yeah. She's a good woman. You said she's a hell of a cook. She makes me feel good—in bed and out." Jasper shrugged and flipped on the high beams. "You know how it is out here, Caleb. I wander around in that big house all by myself. I envy you, really. You have Con to keep you company. Stella was good for you too, kept you in line. But me, well, I've been alone for too long. Sure would be good to have a woman instead of Sebastian to keep my feet warm during the winter. Maybe even pop out a kid or two. Got to have someone to give the place to." He shrugged. "I got nothing to lose."

Caleb stared ahead, not knowing what to say. He very well understood the dilemma his friend was in. They lived the same life, just at different addresses. They farmed and ranched in the middle of God's country. The only break in the monotony was a trip to town to visit friends and family. Caleb wanted someone, too, but was Laura it?

"Your Laura's a looker."

"Yeah," Caleb agreed and took a sip of the coffee he'd bought at the gas station.

"What happened with you and Jenny? Did you take her home that night?"

"Think I'd be bringing Laura tonight if I had?" Caleb shouldn't feel offended. Jasper was one of his closest friends, and he could speak frankly with him. "I followed her home. I saw her to her door and said good night. Not even a kiss. I wasn't even in the mood."

"Hell, no, I bet you weren't." Jasper chuckled. "Not when you had her—" he motioned with a bob of his head toward Laura in the backseat— "waiting for you at home."

"I went to town to get Laura out of my mind. She's my employee, for Christ's sake. I'm still not sure I'm doing the right thing by bringing her along."

"Doesn't look like she's kicking and screaming."

"Not at all. She's along for the ride. I just don't know how far that ride's going to go."

"I reserved three rooms. The two I had for months when they sent out the registration stuff and you told me to save you one. I called last night, and luckily they had a few cancellations, so I booked another room. Figured they could share it, or if Phyllis wanted to bunk with me, Laura could have it."

"I appreciate it, Jasper. I wasn't sure how to bring up the topic with her. This way, she's got a choice." Caleb sighed and closed his eyes.

"Glad to do it. Go on and catch some shuteye. We'll be there before you know it."

Laura rolled onto her stomach, absorbing the last few minutes of sleep in the plush, king-sized hotel bed. Even that expensive, magic number bed she had in her apartment in Chicago wasn't this comfortable. She opened her eyes a crack and caught sight of the clock, surprised it was just after six. She'd slept all of five hours.

Not long after midnight, they'd finally made it to the hotel. She'd slept part of the way, but once they'd stopped for gas and she heard the discussion between Caleb and Jasper, she'd stayed awake, thinking. Caleb had commented to Jasper that he and she were at the point where she'd be comfortable sharing a room with him, and he'd been right. But did he want to share one with her?

She rolled onto her back, stretched her arms above her head, and pointed her toes to the opposite wall. Caleb had told her he'd be over to get her for breakfast at seven-thirty, then registration began at eight. That gave her time to check out the hotel gym, run for a bit on a treadmill, and maybe even sit in the sauna.

She urged herself downstairs and followed through with her plan. She was glad to see a few other women, ladies in much better shape than she was, working out. The cable news station was on, and she felt like she was back home in Chicago working out at the gym. She adjusted the treadmill and started jogging. What had happened to her gym membership? Were they still trying to deduct money from her old, now-empty bank account?

She had literally fallen off the face of the Earth. Was anyone even missing her? Her employees at Bella Vita, no doubt. Anyone else? The miles ticked away, calories burning step-by-step.

When she finished a solid thirty minutes of jogging, she left the exercise room and trailed into the locker room, hoping the sauna would be empty. As she lay on the wood bench, waiting for the steam to clear her pores, she felt her muscles begin to relax.

Caleb was going to drop her off to shop today. She'd get her hair done at one of the salons at the mall, find a pretty dress, and hopefully convince Caleb she was worth more than a few days' worth of his attention.

It sounded like Jasper had some permanent plans for Phyllis, which included moving into his house to be caretaker and cook. Laura would be left as the *last cook standing*, the winner of the competition. She wanted to laugh. If she won by default, at least she would have a job and be on a safe ranch no matter what happened on a personal level between her and Caleb.

Sex and work had never mixed in her world before. Caleb was her boss, and if she slept with him and took care of his son and his house, what would that make her? Would they also start sharing a bed at the ranch? She couldn't, not with Connor; that wouldn't be fair to him. She ran her hands over her face, swiping away the sweat. *Nothing like putting the cart before the horse, Laura.*

More steam drifted in the room, and she was sure she looked like a red beet, but she didn't care. It felt like heaven, and for a few more minutes, she would lounge. When her towel was so heavy that it clung to her body, she decided it was time to get moving.

She put her running gear back on and went to her room. The hallways were empty. Surely some of the other guests and conference people should be up and milling about?

She showered and dressed in her favorite black dress pants and paisley-patterned, wrap-style blouse. She wasn't large in the chest, but the shirt made what she did have look even better. She didn't bother too much with her hair, knowing she would be getting it done, but she did add extra makeup. She was here for Caleb. Her actions would reflect on his reputation, and she didn't want to disappoint him.

With five minutes to spare, she sat on her bed, waiting for Caleb's knock at her door. Surfing the TV channels, she landed back on the news station and groaned at the continued discussion of war and death. Had nothing happy happened overnight?

The knock surprised her, even though she had been expecting it. She shut the television off, grabbed her bag, and opened the door wide. Caleb stood in the hallway, smiling, wearing a nice dress shirt, a tie, and dress pants.

"Wow," she said. "You look great."

"I clean up pretty good, huh?" Caleb turned in a circle for her perusal.

"You sure do." She whistled and took the hand he held out for her, following him into the hallway.

"Are you hungry?" Caleb asked, walking down the hallway with her.

"I worked up an appetite downstairs."

"You worked out today?" he asked. "Even after so few hours of sleep?"

"Don't need much." Laura smiled. "Did you sleep well? It was a longer drive than I thought."

"I think I fell asleep as soon as my head hit the pillow." He opened the breakfast room door for her.

A buffet contained all the expected items, and she quickly filled her plate. They sat at a table for four, expecting Jasper and Phyllis to join them.

"I meant what I said last night." He took a sip of orange juice and swallowed. "Thank you for coming along. It'll be nice to have a dinner date instead of looking at Jasper all night."

"I'm glad to be spending time with you too." She bit into a blueberry muffin.

He reached across the table and took her hand. "I'd like to see how far we can go with this, Laura." His thumb caressed circles on the back of her hand. "I really like you. I thought it was just a passing thing, but my feelings are just getting stronger." He smiled at her. "You're so damn pretty, and I think we can make something from this. What do you think?"

"You look gorgeous," Phyllis said.

Laura modeled her dress in front of the dressing room mirror. They already had their hair done and were trying to decide what to wear for the dinner and dance that evening.

"That's the one, Laura."

Phyllis had chosen her outfit already. It was a bit sedate for Laura's taste, done in a heavy boucle, but Phyllis loved it and decided to go with it. Selective and particular by nature, Laura tried on seven dresses before finally finding one she thought would work. The look on Phyllis's face confirmed Laura's choice.

It was stunning, really. A variation on the simple, black slip dress, this one had layers. The underlay was in a cream-colored satin, covered by small, burned-out velvet circles in an interesting, all-over geometric pattern. It had slim spaghetti straps, a square neckline, and a narrow satin belt that tied lightly at the waist. With a black faux fur wrap and black snakeskin heels to finish the outfit, she knew it was perfect.

"It works." She smiled at her reflection in the mirror.

She really liked the up-do the stylist had fixed. At the salon, they had run into a couple of wives who were here at the conference with their husbands. Both were from Montana, both high maintenance. Laura recognized the wealth, having grown up in such an environment and then later catering to it at the restaurant.

"Okay, set for tonight. Now I need a nice outfit for tomorrow's luncheon, and we can be out of here. Caleb said he'd be back at four, so we have time."

She took off the dress and heels, slipped back into her comfortable blouse and pants, and went to pay for the outfit. The other clothes weren't nearly as difficult to find, and soon, she had another shopping bag full. She found some jewelry to accent the evening dress and felt confident she would shine that evening.

Phyllis charged along, complaining about the shopping. She didn't mind grocery shopping, but the clothing business, well, that was boring to her. Laura, on the other hand, loved to touch the fabrics, play with different looks. Just because she dressed in black more often than not didn't mean she didn't like colors. On the way out, they passed a toy store, and Laura bought Connor two tractors and a small train set.

Jasper was waiting in the pickup, parked in front of the mall. "Did you buy out the stores?" he asked.

They laughed, loading their goods into the back seat. He kissed Phyllis on the lips as she crawled in the front seat next to him, scooting toward the divider. Laura looked away, wanting to give them privacy. They did look like they were in love.

How would it feel to have Caleb look at her like that?

"Caleb wanted to go to another seminar, but he asked that you be ready by five. They're giving us a cocktail hour. Caleb needs to get some more financial backers, Laura. He may not have shared that with you yet, so it might be better that you don't say anything. But he needs to schmooze tonight." Jasper pulled out onto the road, headed back to the hotel.

"Did you find a pretty dress, honey?" He kissed Phyllis's hand and then turned his attention back to the road. "I like your hair. Very nice. I bet you'll be a knockout tonight."

Laura swallowed, feeling like a voyeur.

"Laura helped." Phyllis blushed. "She's got such good taste."

"Well, I think she'll help Caleb's cause tonight. Men like to be around pretty women, and the more men with deep pockets Caleb can visit with, the better off he will be."

Was Jasper telling her indirectly that Caleb was using her as arm candy? Made sense, really. He knew she wouldn't embarrass him, was intelligent enough to carry on a conversation, and could smile prettily. Had she been taken in?

"I thought he had a wealthy backer? Don?"

"He paid Don off with harvest proceeds this year. I think he's looking to move on. Caleb was hoping to have extra to buy some expensive Angus breeding stock. That's the only way his herd will continue to be among the best in the West."

Laura thought about that for a bit. Just how much did a cow cost?

"He's got to line up the money before the end of the year. He and I go to a big stock sale in Denver every January."

"Can't the two of you work together to improve both your herds?" Laura didn't even know enough about cattle to know what she didn't know.

"We do. But it's important to introduce new bloodlines now and again. It strengthens the health of the herd. It's all about the genes."

Laura leaned back in the seat and closed her eyes. She was worth millions. Literally, in a plural sense. Because she hadn't gone into the protection program, the FBI had let her keep it too, which amazed her, but that was part of her tradeoff with the feds. If she did what they wanted, she would get what she wanted. Besides, she'd earned the money honestly, through her hard work and thriftiness.

She sighed. Why the hell was she cleaning toilets when she could be lying on a beach every day for the rest of her life, doing nothing but sipping margaritas from a glass with the paper umbrella hanging out of it, a cabana boy massaging her feet? She laughed. She'd been so used to hard work her whole life, it had never even occurred to her to slack off and take the easy way out.

"What?" Jasper asked, glancing in the rearview mirror at her.

"Nothing." She laughed even harder. "I just had a life-altering thought."

She could leave Nebraska and go to Jamaica and disappear. She had a fake passport ready to go if needed. If Caleb was using her to get financial backing, he wouldn't be overly hurt if she left. Her heart wasn't too involved yet. She glanced at the toy store package resting on the seat next to her and swallowed. Not too involved…yet.

CHAPTER
TWELVE

W HEN FIVE O'CLOCK ROLLED AROUND, Caleb stood outside her
door, looking at her like she was a million dollars, or, at the very
least, a nice Angus bull. It *would* matter if she left him for some
Caribbean island. How had the guy wrapped himself around her heart already?

"Beautiful, Laura, just beautiful."

He moved inside the hotel room door and closed it behind him. His lips
were on hers before she could even wonder what was on his mind. He spun her
around, putting her back against the door.

"Thank you for doing this for me."

"Doing what?" she asked, breathless from the kiss.

"Coming here to a boring beef conference. Keeping me company. Being
you." He kissed her again, the pressure of his lips and taut body pressing
against her.

She could feel his arousal pushing into her stomach. He wanted her,
probably as much as she wanted him.

She pushed him gently away, knowing if they continued, they would miss
the social hour and the networking Caleb so desperately needed. Wanting
a minute to compose herself, she ducked under his arm and went into the

bathroom where she grabbed a pristine white washcloth and came back to a ruffled Caleb.

"Lipstick." She wiped the cloth over his lips, gently removing the lip rouge. "Most men aren't wearing it this season." When she finished, she put the cloth back in the bathroom and looked quickly in the mirror to touch up her own lips.

"We better get going," Caleb said, helping her slip her wrap over her shoulders. "Or I may not leave this room tonight."

"That would kind of hurt your chances of getting financing." She bit her lip after she said it. Jasper had told her not to mention anything.

"What was that?" He frowned at her.

"Isn't that why you're here? To partner with someone to try to better your herd?"

"Yes, it is." He rested his hands on her shoulders and frowned. "But why do you sound so angry about it?"

"I'm not. I just feel a little used, I guess." She fixed her wrap. Not ready to meet his eyes, she double checked that she had her wallet and room key inside her evening bag. "Jasper commented that the best way to get men to talk with you was to have an attractive woman on your arm." She looked up and smiled her most dazzling smile. "Do I fit the bill?"

"You think—" He shook his head and crossed his suit-clad arms over his chest. "Let's get this straight here and now, Laura." He pointed at her. "I asked you along for company. Nothing more. I wanted to get to know you, spend time with you. I don't need a pretty woman to get me what I need."

He opened the hotel door and walked out, not even waiting for her to join him.

"Well, this is a great way to start the evening," she murmured as she chased him down the hall. Dammit to hell, she'd really messed this up.

Jasper and his damn loud mouth. Caleb was so angry the collar of his shirt tightened around his neck. He ran a finger under it, not even caring if Laura was behind him still or a million miles away. She thought he was using her to get money. Of all the stupid things.

"Caleb Kirkpatrick, could you slow down, please?" Laura asked.

He stopped short, and she bumped into his back. He turned around to steady her with his hands.

"Get a room, why don't you?"

He recognized the voice without looking up. When Caleb did look up, he saw Don Peterson, his former partner, strutting down the hall, pulling the waistband of his slacks higher.

"Don." Caleb held out his hand, still holding Laura around the waist.

"I thought I'd try to catch you. Who's your date?" Don looked expectantly at Laura.

"Laura Marshall, please meet Don Peterson."

An odd expression passed across Laura's face. Why was she gritting her teeth? Don didn't seem to notice as he quickly pumped her hand.

"You found yourself a pretty gal this time, Caleb." Don winked. "Are you headed to the happy hour?"

"Yes." Caleb nodded. "Care to join us?"

"Don't mind if I do."

Don led them down the hallway, explaining over his shoulder that he was staying at a different hotel, one with a suite, so he had room to do his wheeling and dealing at the conference.

"I'll buy the first round." Caleb held a chair out for Laura at the table. "What can I get both of you?"

"Whatever you're having," Laura said.

"Whiskey, straight." Don set his cowboy hat on the empty chair at the table.

Caleb watched from the bar, curious what they were talking about. Laura wasn't smiling like she usually did. What was it about Don that bothered her?

The bartender was fast. He took a guess at what she might like and ordered her a glass of white wine. She knew his aversion to liquor, but didn't all women like wine? The whiskey came next and then his glass of pop. The bartender gave him a tray, and Caleb started a tab.

"Bella Vita," Don said, as Caleb set the tray at the table and handed Laura her glass of wine. "That's the restaurant. The best Italian in Chicago." Don took a quick sip and continued. "I was telling your girl that when I'm in Chicago, it's the only place I eat."

"Don travels a lot," Caleb added. "He's got business interests all over the country."

"Chicago is a business hub for certain." She took a sip of wine.

"Well, I find myself there a lot." Don shot a look at Laura, who was staring into her glass, running a finger along the base.

What the hell is wrong with her?

Caleb said, "Denver once a year is plenty enough time in the big cities for me."

"You get used to the size of cities the more you're there. A person finds the hotspots and sticks to what they like." Don finished his whiskey and motioned for another. "What do you like about the ranch so far, Laura?"

"The wide-open spaces. And I don't think I have ever smelled such fresh air."

She sipped on her wine, and Caleb noticed she failed to meet Don's eyes as she answered his question. He decided to ignore his lingering anger from her earlier accusation and placed his hand on her knee. She didn't look his way but instead placed her hand in his.

"What about the animals?" Don asked.

"What about them?" She smiled then, even chuckled a little.

Caleb waved to Jasper and Phyllis as they entered the bar. "You guys are both full of surprises. Who got the woman first?"

"It was a tie." Caleb stood and added a fifth chair to the table for Phyllis.

"Hi, Don." Jasper shook Don's hand and nodded to Caleb.

"You look nice, Phyllis," Caleb said with a smile.

"Thanks." The woman beamed. She'd come a long way in a short time.

Caleb watched Laura closely. From her body language, she wanted to be anywhere but here. Was it their argument that had her in such a mood, or was it the company?

The bell sounded for dinner. They were all in the first seating, so they stood and walked to the door. Caleb put her next to him as he went to settle the bar tab. "I'm sorry I got mad at you," he whispered in her ear and then kissed the area just behind her ear lobe.

"I didn't handle it well, either, I'm afraid." She offered him a smile. "It just hurt to think you might be using me."

"I'm not, Laura." He gave the bartender a twenty and waved off the change. "Well, I may be." He put an arm around her waist and led her to the fancy decorated ballroom. "I guess I'm using you to bring some happiness to my life. Is that okay with you?"

She smiled and nodded. "Let's go eat."

Caleb was surprised by all the people. The room was filled with men wearing all sorts of attire, from jeans and jackets to a couple guys in tuxedoes. The women were all done up in similar fashion to Laura and Phyllis. Caleb and Laura were assigned a table with two other couples already seated. The men half stood as Caleb pulled out Laura's chair, and the women smiled at her.

"Caleb Kirkpatrick." He introduced himself, shaking the men's hands before he sat down. "This is Laura."

Laura nodded and smiled.

"Where are you from, Caleb?" the woman named Kathleen asked, swirling the wine in her glass.

"We're from Nebraska, just north of a town called Mullen. And you?"

"Omaha," Kathleen's husband, Ken, answered.

"Do you farm?" Caleb sipped on his pop.

"We have three sections of ground about an hour northwest of Omaha," the man said. "But we live in the city."

"That's a good-sized operation for around there. Beans and corn?"

The man nodded and took a pull of his beer. "You get to Omaha much?"

Did Caleb look like a country hick? Laura looked like a woman out of a fashion magazine, so even if he appeared backward, she compensated for it. "I go a few times a year. It's a good six-hour drive."

"Oh, Laura," Kathleen groaned. "Where on Earth do you shop?"

"Online, mostly," she answered quietly. "Chicago, every now and then."

Caleb like her nonchalant response. Where he was slightly intimidated by the barrage of questions, she took them in stride.

"Do you have children?" the other lady, Betty, asked.

"A son," Caleb answered before Laura could say no.

"Do you work outside the home?" Kathleen chimed in again.

Why were they so curious about Laura?

"No. Housework and Connor keeps me pretty busy." She offered her a genuine smile.

The waitress came with the bread baskets and salads. She took their order, a choice between steak and chicken. The table quieted for a few minutes as people settled into their plates. He was sure their dining companions thought he and Laura were married, but he didn't care. The wolfish leer the man sitting across from Laura was shooting her way, and the way the man's wife was looking at Caleb, well.... It was probably best they thought Caleb and Laura were married.

"Do you have children, Kathleen?" Laura asked.

"Three," she answered in between bites of sourdough bread. "I work for an attorney, so of course we have a nanny."

"That's convenient." Laura smiled and forked up her salad.

"What part of agriculture are you involved in, Caleb?" Betty's husband, Phil, asked. "Do you have cattle?"

Caleb was glad the topic at the table had turned to more general farming practices. They talked at length about the soil conditions in western Nebraska, how it was easier to grow corn in the east with higher bushel yields.

"I wonder, though," Laura started, "since the land is so much less expensive to purchase and pay taxes on in the west, if it might still be cheaper to grow corn where we are. The bushels per acre are lower, but the overhead is significantly lower too."

Conversation stalled and all of them stared at Laura. She was oblivious, eating her salad, looking down at her plate. She looked up and color flooded her face. "What?"

"Sorry." Ken chuckled. "I'm not used to women talking in those terms, that's all." He laughed again. "Costs are much lower in the west. You folks can't get irrigation, so you don't have the water expenses, and as you said, land values there are lower, so the taxes are lower."

"I imagine if you put the balance sheet side-by-side, they would be comparable." Laura sipped her wine. "The cattle expenses would be similar too, although Caleb has the benefit of BLM leases, where the cattle graze at least part of the year."

Caleb stared at her, thinking he was in a dream. Had she been listening while he and Josh talked at meals? How else would she know what she was saying? She understood it though, even used the correct terminology. He hoped his face didn't give away his shock.

She turned and smiled at him and placed her hand on his thigh.

"Does she do the books, Caleb?" Ken laughed and shoved a fork of salad into his mouth.

"No, but maybe I should consider it, huh?"

"She's not exactly a country hick like you'd expect." A woman's voice echoed off the bathroom tile.

Laura was in the stall, fixing her body shaper, eavesdropping on the conversation between two women who'd come in the bathroom a moment or so after she had.

"Her dress is either a very nice knockoff or she spent a fortune on it."

"I think the latter. She's classy."

"I want to hate her, but I can't. I wish Ken hadn't noticed her. He sat at the table, staring at her throughout the whole meal. Pissed me off. Course, her guy is hot too. Didn't mind looking across the table at him. Think they'd be into it? Wonder how to approach them about it?"

"I don't know. Probably too straight, but you never now. Ken'll get over her. It's just another day, then you go back to Omaha, and they go back to… where was she from again?"

"Mullen, I think the guy said. I don't think they're married. She doesn't wear a ring."

Laura swallowed. The hags were either talking about her or about Phyllis. No one else from Mullen was at the conference. Laura had asked Caleb earlier.

"Then she made all those business comments. Hell, Ken got a hard-on just listening to her talk."

They were referring to her. Now what? She was stuck in a stall. She figured Caleb wouldn't be doing business with the husbands of these women, so what did she have to lose? Dinner was over; Caleb and she wouldn't be sitting with them anymore.

She flushed the toilet, opened the stall door, and walked out. She smiled at the horrified faces in the mirror, washed and dried her hands, checked her lipstick, and walked out, head held high. Let them stew about it.

Caleb was standing in the hallway outside the restroom waiting for her. "Phyllis and Jasper are holding a table for us. The band will start up soon." He took her hand and guided her to a quiet spot at the end of the hallway. He tilted her chin up and looked into her eyes. "You and I will have a discussion tonight. I think I may have underestimated you." He kissed her gently on the mouth. "I think, honey, you are not just a simple cook."

Taking her hand, he guided her back to the main room. Most of the tables had been taken down, and the dance floor was open.

"What's wrong with being a simple cook?" she asked.

"Not a thing. I think my initial impression of you was more accurate though."

"What was that?"

"A very smart woman with things in her past that I very much want to know."

That comment, made casually as he sat her at the table where Phyllis was sitting, twisted her stomach. Don Peterson had recognized her. He ate at Bella Vita every few weeks. He did travel to Chicago often, and she'd talked with him every time he came. She talked to all her patrons when they visited, and as often as he'd been at her restaurant, he and she were on a first-name basis. She might have lost some weight and dyed her hair since she'd last seen him, but surely he had recognized her. Why else would he have brought up her restaurant?

What the hell was she going to do? He was sure to blow her cover, and then what?

So much for the safety of a remote cattle ranch.

"A pretty lady like you shouldn't be sitting here with music ready to start playing."

She hadn't heard Don come up behind her chair. He held out his hand, inviting her to join him. Laura swallowed and smiled, hoping Caleb would say something—anything—but he only nodded in agreement for Don to steal her away.

She put her hand in his and let him lead her out onto the floor. The band was just warming up, playing the slower stuff first, as a larger number of attendees seemed older, probably in their sixties. She fought the cringe she felt as Don placed his hand at the base of her back. She wasn't going to enjoy this dance.

"I'll cut to the chase, pretty girl." He spoke quietly just next to her ear. "You know me. You've talked to me no less than a dozen times at Bella Vita." He turned her smoothly but continued talking. "At first, I thought maybe it wasn't you, but I know you, Sabrina: your smile, your mannerisms. The way you talk to people with your eyes."

"And?" She had tried to prepare for this but hadn't expected such a quick onslaught.

"I heard about the troubles, of course. Your father's murder was plastered all over the *Chicago Trib*. You were out of the restaurant the last time I was in."

Laura nodded, biting down the bile rising up her throat. She was the daughter of the top mob hitman. She was used to rough characters trying to make deals. She hoped she wouldn't have to sell her soul to secure her safety, but she had no idea what Don would expect from her. He had power over her, and that scared her.

"I have to guess that's why you're out here, in the middle of nowhere. You're hiding?"

She nodded again, glancing over at Caleb and meeting his concerned expression with a forced smile.

"You like him?" Don's gaze followed hers.

"More than that." She met his eyes.

"He's the best there is, Sabrina. He'll take good care of you." Don turned her again. "It's not anything like Chicago out here. People don't run spreadsheets and hire lawyers to fight every word of a contract. On a more personal level, they're spontaneous, go with their gut—right or wrong—and seal the deal with a handshake. A boy meets a girl in high school, marries her because she's pretty and her daddy's land borders his daddy's."

"I've realized that already," she said. "They're good, honest people out here."

"A simple life is sometimes the best life."

She nodded, thinking about how her life had changed in the blink of an eye. The greed and power struggles that controlled and ultimately led to the destruction of her father and his associates.

"Was your pop's murder mob related?"

She nodded and swallowed.

"Garbaldo?"

She looked up into his eyes, surprised at the gentle expression on his face. She glanced away, touched by his concern, and looked at the band, blinking her eyes quickly, hoping her legs would still hold her up, as shaky and wobbly as she was feeling.

"Are you involved with him?" she whispered, afraid he would say yes.

"Hell, no!" He laughed. "All my business is legit and aboveboard. Just as your Bella Vita was."

She nodded again, forgetting the stomach issues and worrying instead that tears might start to fall. How the hell would she explain that? "The FBI suggested Nebraska. I'm not officially in their protection program, but if I find myself in need, I have a contact."

"What about your restaurant?"

"I had to give up Bella." She sniffed, her eyes tearing up more.

"I was there again last week. It's not quite the same. No pretty dark-haired, blue-eyed smiling lady welcoming me, checking on my meal. But I guess I know where I can find you."

"You won't tell anyone?"

He shook his head. "Not if you make me a deal."

What the hell did the man want? He was holding her future, possibly her life in his hands. "A deal?"

"I thought about this earlier after our drinks, through dinner. How was I going to get you to talk to me? I've always really liked to you. I've known you for almost six years, you know. Not that we were friends, but I had something to look forward to every time I came to the Windy City."

"It's kind of you to say that, Don." She looked back at him. "What are your terms?"

He laughed. "Don't look so worried; it's nothing you can't handle. You need to tell Caleb who you really are. Especially if your heart is going to get involved with him. That's the first part."

"I had planned to. Your appearance just sped up the need to do so."

She looked back at Caleb. He was talking with Phyllis and Jasper.

"What else?" she asked.

"How about you agree to make me sweet potato gnocchi the next time I come out to the ranch? They don't serve it at Bella anymore."

"I know it's your favorite." She smiled, feeling less worried about her secret getting out. But could she trust this guy? "I took the recipe with me when I left. You're welcome to supper anytime. Just give me a little heads-up."

"Since I've met your mother and we've talked about it before, I sort of know how much money you're worth. At least ballpark. Unless the FBI froze your assets?"

She shook her head, skeptical. "They couldn't prove any of that money came from illegal means. Because it didn't." Did he expect a payoff?

"Invest it in Caleb," he said. "He won't take any more money from me. Paid me off three years before we agreed. He's definitely motivated to expand and grow, so he's got something for his kid, unlike what his dad did to him and Josh."

Sounded as if there was a story there, but she would wait and ask Caleb about that.

"Think he'd use my money?" she asked quietly.

"Make it a wedding gift." The song ended. He laughed at her expression and kissed her cheek. "You've made him happy already."

Don led her back to Caleb who was standing, waiting for her.

CHAPTER
THIRTEEN

"I DON'T USUALLY DANCE." CALEB PULLED her closer to him. She smelled like flowers, light and airy. Laura's hand fit perfectly in his as he guided her around the floor. "I just really wanted to touch you, and this is the only appropriate way to do so."

"Well, I'm glad to be in your arms." She said moved in even closer.

He never danced. Not here, not at the bar in town. But tonight, he wanted to. He wanted to be close to her.

"Did Don upset you?" He bent his head and whispered in her ear. He wanted to kiss her but held back.

"No." She shook her head. "He just reminded me that I have things to talk about with you tonight."

"How's that?" Caleb pulled back so he could look into her eyes.

"I have known Don for a few years."

"You have?" He was worried when she wouldn't meet his gaze. He let go of her hand and tipped up her chin, so she could look at him.

"The restaurant he mentioned?" She raised her eyebrows. "Bella Vita?"

Caleb nodded, recalling Don talking about it earlier at the bar.

"That was my restaurant."

Her restaurant? Like, she worked there or it belonged to her? People around them were noticing they had stopped moving to the music. He resumed dancing with her.

"Really? Well, what a small world."

He decided to let it drop until later when they were alone and in his hotel room, a glass of wine in her hand. He imagined it would be a long story, and it hurt his gut to even imagine what she would be telling him. He urged himself not to think the worst of them; it was probably just an innocent acquaintance.

"Did you have any luck with your schmoozing?" she asked.

"I haven't done much. I can't seem to keep my eyes off you." He laughed and gave her a hug as the song ended.

Ken, the man they'd had dinner with, was waiting at their table for them. "Caleb, think we could talk business for a bit?" he asked before they even sat down.

"Sure. You bet."

Ken glanced at Laura.

"Honey, maybe you could go freshen up?"

"No problem." She smiled and nodded, grabbed her bag, and left the hall.

When they were alone, Ken started right in. There wasn't room for small talk in this discussion. Apparently, he had something on his mind.

"Coupla of guys were commenting on the quality of your herd. You planning to sell off some bulls come spring? I could start with the cow-calf pairs too."

"I thought you were just a crop farmer." Caleb sipped on his watered-down pop. "I didn't know you had livestock."

"Well, that Don Peterson, he speaks pretty highly of your herd." Ken motioned to the waitress for another drink. "I've considered for a coupla years diversifying with livestock. Prices have been good on beef lately. Figure it's a good time to jump in."

"Sure," Caleb agreed. Ken was right. It was a good time to get into beef, which was why he needed to add to his herd.

"Do you and your woman swing?" Ken's voice had dropped low.

"Country *swing?*" Caleb nodded. "She likes to dance, not me so much."

"No, I mean *swing.*" He lowered his voice even further and leaned forward. "*Wife swap?* My wife and I decided to try it when we go to conferences like this. Gives you something to look forward to when you see the same people year after year."

"You've got to be kidding?" Caleb laughed, still struggling to wrap his mind around what Ken was saying. He had to be joking.

"It's a hell of a lotta fun. You know these conferences can get kinda dull."
Ken shook his head. "Makes things more interesting in the bedroom, if you
know what I mean." He elbowed Caleb. "'Course, with Laura, I bet things are
always interesting. She's got those legs that go on forever."

Caleb swallowed, thinking he needed to slug the bastard.

"Excuse me." Caleb stood so fast the chair tipped sideways.

"Wait! I'm sorry." Ken grabbed Caleb's arm to hold him there. "I just
thought maybe I would ask. You never know who's into what. I'd still like to
talk business. Maybe tomorrow?"

"Probably not." Caleb looked over the ballroom and saw Laura talking
to Phil's wife. Was she propositioning Laura too? What a whacked-out world
they lived in. Too bizarre and complicated for a country boy like him. Wife
swap? He would never in a million years let another man touch Laura.

And that possessiveness spoke volumes.

"Do you know what she asked me? I thought she was joking!" Once they were
clear of the ballroom, Laura burst out laughing. He'd come to her rescue just
in time. "Kathleen asked if I would sleep with her husband. She wanted to
watch him *do it* with me." She stopped and leaned against the wall, just next
to the elevator, sure she was as flushed as a tomato. "She told me he'd spoken
of nothing else since dinner but making love to me…actually, *swapping*." She
giggled. "You'd get her after she was done watching. Can you believe it?"

"I can."

"What?" she squealed, her eyes narrowing. "Caleb?"

"That's how I've felt since I met you, Laura. You've turned me into mush."

He leaned into her and kissed her, holding her lips until the elevator
doors opened. An older couple stepped off the elevator.

Laura and Caleb stepped on, and as soon as the doors closed, Caleb
pushed her up against the wall, opening her mouth with his tongue. One hand
remained against the wall, supporting him, while the other one rested on her
waist, holding her against him. They arrived at their floor too soon, and the car
came to a stop. He pulled away, rubbing his thumb gently over her lips.

How did he do that? With a simple, gentle kiss he made her hot.

"Your room or mine?" He took her hand and strolled with her down the hall.

She looked at him, caught his wink, and smiled. "Mine. Then I can kick
you out before it goes too far."

"How far is that?" he whispered, flashing her a wolfish grin.

"I'll let you know."

She slipped the plastic key card in the slot, and when the door clicked, pulled down on the handle, and they went inside. Laura flipped on the light. The maid had straightened since Laura had last been in there.

"So, shall we talk first or do you want to fool around?" He pulled his tie free and let it hang around his neck.

She slipped off her heels and tossed her wrap and handbag on the chair by the window. He hung his suit coat over the same chair and sat on the edge of the bed. She remained standing, uncertain of what to do next.

"You're beautiful, Laura." He held out a hand and pulled her onto the bed next to him. "'Course you don't need me to tell you that."

"It makes me feel good though, so don't stop, okay?" She leaned forward and kissed him. Her hands cupped his face and held him tightly. She meant it to be gentle, and it was. She pulled away and stared at him. "I like you a whole lot, Caleb. I think you're awfully handsome." She joined her lips with his again before she pulled away and crossed her arms at her chest.

"Shall we play our question game again?" Caleb asked.

Could he sense her nervousness? It was easy and fun to be bold and clever when they could only go so far. A hotel room with a big bed was a different story. Was he as unsure of this as she was?

"I think you probably have more for me tonight, so maybe I'll just sit in the hot seat?"

"Okay." He bent over and untied his shoes and pulled them off.

It was oddly arousing and intimate to see the man in his stocking feet. He took off his tie completely, threw it on their heap of clothing, and unbuttoned the top buttons of his shirt, showing the light, dusting of hair she'd been hoping to find. He stood up and went to the head of the bed to fluff up the pillows. He sat back down and stretched out his legs in front of him.

"Getting comfy, are you?" Laura chuckled. "That's the side I sleep on."

"Me, too. I guess we'll have to do rock, paper, scissors for it."

"How about a thumb-wrestling match." She giggled, making a fist and wiggling her thumb at him.

"I'd cream you." He laughed and patted the area next to him on the bed.

"Probably." She sighed dramatically. "Okay, I know there are two things for sure you want to know about. What I am other than a cook." She counted on her fingers. "And why I know Don."

"Right on both counts." He nodded. "I've got more, but that will be a good start."

"Which first?"

"Education."

"Okay." She cozied up next to him, crossing her legs in front of her, admiring her fresh pedicure through her pantyhose. "That's easy. I went to Catholic schools from kindergarten through high school. I got a full ride to Notre Dame, where I majored in finance and business econ." She wiggled her feet, surprised how much shorter her legs were than his. "The summer after I graduated, I went to the Culinary Institute in New York." She laughed. "I feel like I'm in a job interview."

"Don't, Laura. It's just the way you spoke at dinner, I knew there was more to your talents than what you can do in the kitchen. I noticed that too, when you asked about inventory and ordering. Most cooks would only care if they had ingredients, not how much they cost or even how they got them to the ranch."

"Most of my cooking ability came down from my great grandma—Nonna Vita. The institute gave me the polish I could get only at a cooking school. That fall, I started my MBA at Northwestern. The next fall, I opened Bella Vita." She shrugged. "I worked my tail off, never missed a night at the restaurant until my pop died."

"When was that?"

His face was hard to read. Laura was putting all her cards on the table for this man, another person who would hold power over her head.

"A few months ago."

She was glad he let that hang for the moment. She figured she'd be forced to go into greater detail in the near future.

"So, you chucked all that for Nebraska?" He shook his head and pulled her against him. "Not sure that was your best decision. I think, in your grief, you ran away."

"There's more to the story, I'm afraid." She twisted herself, so she was no longer lying next to him but instead sat facing him. "That's where Don comes in."

"He met you at your restaurant." He rested his hand on her thigh. "You told me. But what I can't figure out is why you didn't act like you knew him when we were sitting at the bar together? Did you have a relationship with him?"

"Heavens, no!" she barked. "He's older than my dad was. At least, I think so." She sat up straighter and arranged her dress, so she could cross her legs without flashing her panties. She took his hands. "This may sound off-the-wall, but if you don't believe me, Don can back up the story."

"Sounds ominous."

"Pop was murdered." She started slowly, thinking through her choice of words as she went. "For all my life, or at least as long as I can remember, Pop was a runner for a man named Ernesto Garbaldo, who, for all intents and purposes, ran a gangster family in Chicago. He isn't the biggest gun, by any means, but he's still damn influential."

"And that's who murdered him? You know that?"

"Yes, we know that." She swallowed, remembering the scene outside the courthouse, the pain that seared her flesh as the small bullet went into her back and out through her side. "We don't know which man actually pulled the trigger." She shook her head. "That, probably no one will ever know. But the problem is Pop, my sister, my mother, and I all ratted out Ernesto just days before Pop was murdered. The FBI told us we needed to make ourselves scarce, but Pop didn't disappear fast enough."

She met Caleb's eyes, taken aback by the shock on his face. "They found the job at the Morning Glory, had me contact your brother, who *sort of* interviewed me, and the next thing I knew, I was on a plane headed for Omaha."

"Wow, that's quite the story."

"It's all true." Laura nodded for emphasis. "Pop made the newspapers. I've got a gunshot wound in my back if you want to see."

"They shot you too?" He pulled away, anger etched on his face.

"I got in the way. I was with Pop. We even had agents all around us, protecting us, and they still got us."

"This is incredible, Laura."

"The story of my life." She ran her hands along her naked arms, feeling a chill. "I just wish it were fiction."

"Are you cold?" He reached out to touch her arm.

"I might get changed, if that's okay with you." She shimmied off the bed. "You didn't want to go dance anymore, did you?"

"Nope." He shook his head. "Go ahead and change. Maybe you want me to leave?"

"No!" She rushed to answer him. "Unless you want to, now you've heard my tale?"

He shook his head.

"Maybe you want me to leave the ranch?" She hoped she knew the answer. "As long as Don is trustworthy, I'm not in any danger out there—and neither is your family."

"He is. I don't want you to leave. Just understand this is a lot for me to absorb."

"I know. It was for me, too."

Damn, what a surprise. Caleb shook his head. How the hell was he supposed to react to all this? He believed every word she said, knew she spoke the truth, but who would have thought she was involved in such a mess? He watched her grab clothes from her suitcase and walk into the bathroom to change.

He leaned his head back on the wooden headboard and rested a hand on his forehead. He still wanted her; if anything, his protective nature was coming out. He could trust Don, but to be sure, Caleb would have a discussion with his old business associate the next day.

"What's your real name?" he asked as soon as she walked out of the bathroom. She was dressed in a pair of jeans and a low-cut sweater that hugged her curves. Her hair was free from the fancy hairdo she'd worn for dinner and dancing. She looked real…and incredibly sexy.

"I don't look like a Laura Marshall?" She hung her dress on a hanger and hooked it on the clothes rack near the door before crawling back onto the bed.

"No, you look too Italian to be a Marshall."

"I wonder what nationality Marshall is? English, maybe? I probably should have studied that a little more." She laughed. "The name I was given at birth was Sabrina Rose Marconi. Everyone called me Bre."

"That suits you better," he said, holding her next to him. "Anything else I need to know? Still a virgin?"

"Not quite," she admitted with a chuckle. "Catholic girls might start too late, to quote that song, but I did make a couple of bad choices along the way."

"Well, there are a few in my past too." He reached for her. "I know any other man wouldn't be able to hold back with you in bed, but I want our first time to be special. Should I call you Bre?"

"Better stick to Laura, and I think we're okay with the waiting too. I wouldn't mind cuddling with you in front of the television though. How about it?"

"Come here, then." He took the remote from the bedside table and turned on the television. He raised his arm and pulled her underneath.

Her body curved next to his, and she rested her head back on his shoulder. They didn't know each other very well, but he felt a connection to her. He reminded himself of his vow not to get too entangled with a woman—that they bring heartache—but he wasn't going to let the thought ruin the moment. There was a long way between what they were sharing and a lifetime commitment.

"Why don't you drink?" she asked quietly when a commercial came on.

He'd chosen the History Channel, which was showing a Halloween special about haunted houses in the West. He'd always been fascinated by such things. Before the commercial, they'd featured a haunted saloon outside of Denver.

"Personal choice." He was purposely vague. She may have opened up to him, but he wasn't quite ready to let go of all his secrets yet.

"I was surprised when you ordered wine for me at the bar."

"Don't most women like wine?"

"Yes, I think so; at least, at the restaurant they seemed to. I'm not much of a drinker though." She reached across his lap and grabbed his hand. "I had a few lousy years in college when I had a real problem with the stuff. I avoid it most of the time now."

"What got you to quit?" He met her gaze with a steady look.

"I was flunking one of the core business classes. I had to make up a test on a Friday morning, so I studied at the library on a Thursday instead of going to the frat house I'd been hanging out at, and I know it sounds weird, but I finally got it. I knew if I didn't clean up, I would end up a runner for the mob. Or worse."

"You knew what your folks did wasn't right? I mean, even though you grew up in it, you knew it was wrong?"

She nodded. "I've lived a really clean life since then. I haven't had sex since then either. So I was pretty glad when you asked to wait." She covered her face with her hands. "I can't believe I'm telling you all this. You're my boss, and I hardly even know you!"

"I might be your boss, but I think we know it's a hell of a lot more than that." He leaned over and kissed her forehead, pulling her close. "Thank you for sharing. For trusting me with your secrets."

She pulled back a bit and turned back to the television. He could tell she was uncomfortable by what she'd shared. He wished he had the guts to tell her his story, but he wasn't ready yet. He wasn't ready to open himself up that far.

"We're missing the popcorn," she told him with a chuckle. "Need popcorn for a good ghost story."

Pounding woke Laura up. The room was dark, and for a minute, she thought she was dreaming. Then she realized she was still at the hotel, and someone was banging on her door. She felt the bed, trying to remember when Caleb left her. He was gone, and her heart raced, scared who would be at the door.

Had Ernesto found her? Did Don lie about knowing him? She'd been so damn careful and now....

"Laura?"

She felt for the light on the bedside table and turned it on as she heard Caleb calling to her. It was three in the morning. What the hell was going on?

She sighed and crawled from the bed, the adrenaline from the sudden fear subsiding. She wasn't in danger. Still in her jeans and sweater, she went to the door.

"Coming." She looked through the peephole.

Caleb stood in the corridor wearing a T-shirt and sweats. She rushed to open the door and welcomed him inside.

"What happened? Why are you all wet?" she asked.

She looked down the hallway. Several other people were milling about.

"The sprinklers must have malfunctioned. I came to see if yours were going off too." He wheeled in his bag and hung his suits in the closet.

She shut the door and looked around. "I guess not." She looked down at his case. "Did your suitcase get all wet? Do you have something to change into?"

"I had it closed and it's waterproof, so I think everything is safe."

"Well, change already; you'll catch a cold." She waved him toward the bathroom. "You can sleep here tonight, and we'll sort it out in a few hours."

She crawled back into bed and snuggled into the small spot she'd already warmed. He joined her a few minutes later, hard and warm as he spooned her body. "Thanks for letting me share your bed."

His breath was warm at her ear, and she held his hand wrapped at her waist.

"You're welcome. Just don't hog the covers."

"They did what?" Laura stepped out of the bathroom, wearing her conservative, terrycloth robe, which concealed the racy undergarments Phyllis had convinced Laura to buy at the mall the day before. A thong, of all things, and an amazing lacy bra. The tile floor was cold on her bare feet, and her hair was still dripping water droplets from the shower.

"Jasper said in his voicemail that they were flying out of Casper early this morning for Vegas." He glanced at his watch. "They're probably in Salt Lake City already. They decided to get married! They'll be back tomorrow morning before we leave for home. They plan to ride back to the ranch with us."

"Wow." She holding her toothpaste-loaded toothbrush, she turned back to the bathroom sink. She looked in the mirror and proceeded to follow her morning ritual. It was odd though, knowing he was watching. Not so much the makeup-free face—he'd seen that every morning before she'd gone for a run. More the intimate, standing-in-a-robe, brushing-the-teeth-barefoot thing.

"Help yourself to the shower," she said. "I even left you a towel."

She jumped when he lightly pinched her side on his way past.

Phyllis was getting married this morning. How strange to hop on a plane, fly to Vegas, and get hitched at some flowery, cheesy wedding chapel. But people did it all the time. She looked in the mirror, wiped the toothpaste off her cheek, and left the small bathroom. It was pretty romantic really. She hoped it worked out for them.

The water was running in the tub; she could hear him in the shower. Laura figured it was safe to get dressed. She pulled out one of the new outfits she'd bought the day before at the mall.

The thought of him naked in the shower was playing havoc with her senses. Scenes from an old daytime soap opera she used to watch in college filtered through her head, and she remembered how the heroine seduced her man by climbing in behind him, soaping his wet back, his bottom, his…. She sighed. Would she ever have the guts to do such a thing?

Caleb had taken her news in stride, hadn't even seemed the least bit skeptical. Maybe it wasn't an issue, like Laura had imagined it would be. First Don and now Caleb; two levelheaded men found the situation odd but accepted it.

When the shower turned off, she panicked and grabbed her bag. He would be coming out, probably wearing a little towel the hotel wrongly assumed would be large enough to wrap around the waist of a normal-sized person. She would run downstairs and grab coffee, giving him some privacy to dress.

Before she could leave, he cracked open the bathroom door and called out, "Are you decent?"

She chuckled. "Are you?"

"I've covered my privates." He walked into the main room. "The towel doesn't leave much room for anything else."

"Wow." Looking better than any half-naked fireman she'd seen on the calendars her sister hung up each year in their shared bathroom growing up,

Caleb stood in front of her with wet, mussed hair and a towel that covered his waist and little else. His chest, from neck to the waist, was covered in curly brown hair. Laura stared in surprise. She hadn't imagined he'd have so much hair. She couldn't stop looking at him.

"Talk about beautiful." She sighed.

"Stop staring," he commanded with a laugh. "You're embarrassing me."

He walked to his suitcase, the towel parting, and she could see the uppermost part of his thigh. He was amazing, all muscle. Time to leave.

"I...um...I'll go get some coffee." The door stuck as she tried to flee, but she got it open and hurried out of the room.

He was covered, just not as much as she would have liked. Well, that wasn't quite true. She would have liked him to be wearing less if she was honest with herself.

The soap opera heroine would have had fun with that. "Beautiful man in a skimpy towel—take one." Of course, on the soap opera, they would still be in the shower.

She laughed at herself as she walked down the hallway, squishing on the wet carpet. The whole length of the hallway was wet, all the way to the elevator. It wasn't standing water; the carpet had sucked it up like a sponge. A shame, really. It was a nice hotel.

She took the stairs to the main level, where the breakfast room was located.

Inside, Don was sitting at a table, reading one of the national papers. She filled two cups of coffee, grabbed two small creamers and some sugar, and walked back to say hello to him.

"How are you this morning?"

"Fine, fine," he said, standing.

"Sit, please." She smiled. "I was just getting coffee and going back up. I thought you were staying at a different hotel."

"I am, but I was supposed to meet someone this morning for business talk." He folded his paper and set it aside. "You might be interested in one of the afternoon presentations today."

"Me? Really?" She frowned. "What's the topic?"

"It's a three-hour seminar on the basics of organics. Beef, vegetables. I've always admired that actor's line of organic food." Don leaned back in his chair and crossed his arms. "He does sauces and packaged food. I was thinking there was a pretty strong market for it, too, especially in the metropolitan areas with people who are more health-conscious. The millennial generation. With your recipes and a good, organic-food base, you could make a killing in the market. The biggest organic food store is merging with the largest online retailer. I expect the market to become huge."

"You mean *we* could make a killing, don't you?" She chuckled. "I thought about doing a cookbook with my great grandma's recipes but never considered pre-packaged stuff. I did a lot of carry-out and premade meals at the restaurant."

"Well, if you're interested, I'll be there. Maybe we could cook up something together?"

"Clever pun, Don." She rolled her eyes and patted his shoulder.

"I love your cooking. That's really an understatement." He laughed and leaned back on his chair. "Organics is a food concept I want to explore. I have connections to some of the larger food processors. Ones in Omaha, even. Maybe Caleb would consider growing some of the veggies?" He shrugged. "It's worth a pitch to them."

She paused, considering, and then nodded.

"I'll see you after lunch," she said and walked out.

What a boon she'd just been handed! Live in the middle of nowhere, develop tasty, ready-made food, and then construct a cookbook. Using organics. She had used organics at her restaurant on a limited basis. The cost was prohibitive on the meats, but her tomatoes were all hydroponically raised.

Things were looking better by the minute.

CHAPTER

FOURTEEN

"THANKS, HONEY." CALEB TOOK THE coffee cup from her hand and a packet of sugar. "I called Con while you were gone, caught him just before he and Mom were going to school." He sat at the built-in desk next to the window.

"Is he having fun with Grandma?" The edge of the bed was the only other option in the room, so she sat down.

"Seems to be." He took a sip and rested the cup on his knee. "He asked if you bought him something."

"Oh! Yeah, I forgot to tell you, I did stop at a toy store." She stood up and walked to the pile of bags and pulled out a colorful one and handed it to him. "I got him a couple of things. Thought you could give him the truck…well, grain cart, I guess. I don't know all these farm machines." She laughed.

Why did she have to be so damn perfect? He stared at her as she handed him the bag. He looked inside, noting how she had hit the nail right on the head when it came to Connor's taste in toys. Beautiful, sexy, smart, and funny. He'd be a fool not to pursue this relationship, even though she was in hiding and could potentially disappear from his life. His heart had never been touched by a woman like she was affecting him. Even early on with Christie, he'd known it wouldn't be a permanent, heart-bending thing. Laura, on the other hand….

"What?" she asked quietly, sitting back on the bed and taking a sip of her coffee.

"Just thinking. I'm missing your cooking, I think. Biscuits and gravy is what I'm wishing for right now." He chuckled into his coffee cup, taking another sip.

"Since Phyllis will be cooking for someone else now, you'll probably get pretty sick of my cooking soon enough." She sipped again.

"I doubt that," he answered truthfully. "I've already put on a little extra weight since you came out here."

"Where? In your big toe?" She smirked. "You could always bring out a few more women to compete against me? See if I'm still the best choice?"

"Funny girl, why would I go and do that?" He set his coffee cup on the desk and leaned forward, his elbows resting on his knees. "Do you want to take the pickup today? Check out more of Casper?"

"Actually, I was wondering…. Do you think the conference would let me sit in a meeting or two? I met Don downstairs, and he suggested one this afternoon I might like."

"Which one?" He felt stupid, not even having considered she might be interested in the meetings.

"Organics, at one o'clock."

"I hadn't planned to sit in on that one, but sure, why not? What about this morning? Maybe you'll be interested in something?"

"What are the choices?"

He pulled out the program brochure and handed it to her. He'd marked a few things he wanted to check out. The last day was always more casual but also more frenzied. He still had two men he wanted to discuss his herd plans with, provided he was presented with an opportunity.

For lunch, Bud Rawlings, one of the larger breeders in Montana, waved Caleb and Laura to join him at his table. His very pregnant wife, Sarah, smiled at Laura and patted the seat next to her. Caleb and Bud had met years earlier at the National Cattlemen's Association meeting in Colorado and immediately formed a friendship, continued through frequent emails and occasional phone calls.

"How much longer do you have to go?" Laura asked Sarah, placing her napkin on her lap.

"Just three weeks or so. My doctor would flip if he knew I'd come down here. My last two babies were early." Sarah shifted uncomfortably on the chair.

"I wish you the best of luck." Laura grinned.

The lunch conversation then revolved around family. Caleb talked about Connor and the Rawlings about their four boys. Sarah said she was hoping for a girl this time; they had decided to be surprised. Bud knew Josh, so Caleb told them Holly was expecting too.

Caleb's attention was divided. He was trying to figure out how to fit in the discussion of expanding from simple friendship to a business arrangement with Bud...if Laura's laugh didn't distract him. He was trying to listen to the conversation she was having with Sarah and still keep up with Bud.

"Are you in a rush to get back?" Laura asked him, eyeing the dessert cart the waiter brought by the table.

"No." He laughed. "Do you plan on taking a long time to eat one of those?"

"Oh, no. I could inhale it if needed." She pointed to something chocolate.

He chose a cherry cheesecake.

"I make a good cheesecake," she said after the waiter left.

"You like to bake?" Sarah asked, cutting into her pie.

"I do." Laura nodded. "I'm Caleb's cook at the ranch."

"Oh!" Sarah exclaimed. "I thought you two were...involved. You're so comfortable with each other."

"Just the cook." Laura focused on her dessert.

Her statement bothered him, hit him deep in the gut. But it was true, wasn't it? They hadn't established any relationship. A little snuggling and a few kisses didn't make him her boyfriend. But maybe that was what bugged him? He wanted to be more than her employer.

"Do you do organics at all, Bud?" Laura asked, no doubt thinking about the next meeting they would be going into.

"No." He shook his head. "We are traditional grass-fed Angus, just like Caleb's ranch. Some of the best, if I say so myself, but not organic." He wiped his mouth. "For us, it would be too difficult to switch. Too costly. I think we'd have to change to an all-corn-fed program and organic feed, at that. The cost would be astronomical, at least early on. Studies are still inconclusive about any superiority in organics, so we haven't seen much reason to change."

Caleb looked her way and noticed her studying Bud. "Have you and Caleb worked together on breeding programs?" She turned to Caleb. "Isn't that what you call it?"

Bud laughed and wiped his mouth. He took a sip of water before he answered. "Where are you from, Laura?"

"Chicago."

"Well, for a city girl, you sure can talk the talk."

He and Sarah both laughed, but not unkindly.

"Caleb and I haven't done any business together, no." Bud turned his gaze back to Caleb. "I was thinking we should discuss swapping a bull or two if you're interested. Or I'll buy one from you, if you'd rather. Mix it up a bit." He leaned back on his chair and crossed his arms. "I thought about heading to Dallas to the stock show, but with the baby coming, I'd rather stay close to Sarah." He took his wife's hand and squeezed it. "I talked with Manfred, and he told me you're trying to improve your stock too. So, what do you say? I think it would be good for both of us."

Caleb smiled. This couldn't have worked out better if he'd planned it ahead of time. Laura was his lucky charm and apparently a damn good listener and quick learner, at least when it came to the agriculture business

"Thank you," Caleb told Laura as soon as they were in traffic and on the way back to the hotel and conference center.

"For what?" She was genuinely confused.

"I'm not sure how you did it." He glanced over his shoulder to switch lanes. "For three years at this conference, I've been trying to work up the courage to ask Bud to swap livestock with me. I've wanted some of his cattle for as long as I can remember, but I never quite got the nerve to bring it up."

Caleb looked sheepishly at Laura. It surprised her he was shy about such a thing. That had to be an integral part of his business.

"Don't you like the wheeling and dealing?"

He turned to her and shook his head. "Not much intimidates me, you understand." He focused back on the busy road in front of them. "I rode bulls on the rodeo circuit for ten years or more. Those huge beasts didn't scare me, but trying to convince Bud or anyone of his caliber to work with me is intimidating."

"You don't strike me as shy," she said, looking out the window.

"I am," he admitted. "It comes from growing up where I did. How I did."

"I see."

"Not really, Laura." He glanced her way again and then back at the road with a shake of his head and a sigh that sounded so deep, as if it came from his toes. "Like you, I have a few skeletons. Mine, however, are best left in the closet."

"Everyone has things they'd rather not have done, Caleb."

She touched the back of his hand, which was resting on his thigh, and he turned it so he could entwine his fingers with hers.

"Maybe so." He squeezed her hand.

They drove for more than ten minutes in silence, while Laura considered what he'd just admitted. Marketing and haggling were always a fun challenge for her when she had the restaurant. Would she be overstepping herself by offering to help him with it?

That morning, before lunch, they'd sat through two presentations geared toward the sales and marketing perspective of the ranching industry. Caleb had filled pages of paper with notes. She, on the other hand, realized she could have given the presentations.

Without using notes as a guide.

She knew Caleb had a great talent with the animals, skill with planning the crops and harvesting. She had no idea about that aspect of the industry. But marketing.... Well, that she excelled at. She was about to ask how he marketed the crops when they reached the hotel.

The parking lot was crowded, but he found a spot near the main entrance. Laura moved to open her door, but Caleb was quicker, drawing her to him in a quick, passionate kiss. He pulled his mouth slowly away and then held her for several minutes before leaning back on his seat.

"Do you really think all you are to me is the ranch cook?" he asked.

"Aren't I?"

"For a smart girl, you sure are blind." He leaned in again and kissed her. He backed up just enough to meet her eyes. "You stopped being just a cook the night I came home to find you lying on my couch, taking care of Connor. You care about him, and that means the world to me."

"Okay, so I'm the cook and the nanny." She shrugged, comfortable with that notion but hoping he would say something that would make her heart melt.

"You're more than that, Laura, I care about you, and I'd like.... Well, I'd like to be *involved* with you." He caressed her cheek with the back of his fingers.

"What does *involved* mean to you?" She tried not to hold her breath as she waited for the answer.

His laugh caught her off guard. "I'm not sure. If this was like thirty years ago, I suppose I would ask you if you wanted to go steady."

"Oh." She swallowed. "Do I get to wear your class ring and letter jacket?" The chuckle erupted from her without warning.

"If you want." He shrugged. "I think I still have both."

"What other...perks...come with this 'going steady' business?" She leaned in this time, placing a soft, gentle kiss at the hollow of his neck.

"Well, there's this." He tilted her head up to meet his lips, this time deeper, more intensely. "Even more if you want. We'll go slowly, Laura. The last thing I want is to ruin a good thing."

"Is that what I am? A good thing?"

"Isn't that what that Martha cooking gal always said about her best cooking ideas? It's a good thing? And you, Laura, are a very good thing."

"I didn't know you had such an interest in organics," Caleb commented when he finally got a word in.

Laura hadn't stopped talking about the presentation they'd sat through that afternoon. Don had invited them to join him for dinner at the Mexican restaurant he claimed was the best in the West.

"I didn't before today." She munched on her taco salad, moving the lettuce around in the baked tortilla bowl to pick up the last drips of salsa. "It's fascinating."

"So are you in?" Don asked with a chuckle.

"What do you mean, is she in?" Caleb looked between the two, knowing he was missing something.

"I suggested to her this morning, when she came to fetch coffee, that she consider creating a line of Italian premade organic dinners. You know I work with that processor out of Omaha. I told her I'd pitch it to them."

"I see." He frowned. "She didn't tell me." He shifted his gaze to Laura as he bit into his third taco. "No wonder you're so excited about the topic."

It reminded him, rather abruptly, that she was so much more than a cook. He realized that were he in her world, the world of Chicago and high finance, she might not even have given him a second look.

"It has possibilities. I always hoped to put my great grandma's recipes in a cookbook. As a matter of respect for her. She taught me all I know in the kitchen."

Don laughed and wiped sauce off the corner of his mouth. "I knew you didn't learn it from your mother. She's a knockout but never struck me as domestic."

Laura laughed and agreed with a nod.

Caleb suddenly felt like a third wheel. She and Don had a past. Maybe not a friendship, but he knew enough about her real life to be able to understand her, converse with her. And now Don was considering including her in a business venture.

As if sensing his discomfort, she put her hand on his thigh and squeezed. He made a face he hoped looked like a grin.

"Interested in growing organic veggies for me?" She sipped on her nonalcoholic margarita.

"I'm pretty set in my ways. Like Bud said this morning, it would take a lot of expensive changes to make it work."

"How much does land cost around you?"

"Thinking of trying your hand at agriculture?"

"Nope, I'll leave that to the pros." She smiled. "I thought maybe I could hire it out, have someone work the land for me." She shrugged and bit into the shell of the taco salad. "I guess it would be the processor who had to find the ingredients, anyway, not me."

Caleb didn't want the conversation to go any further. Laura was a spitfire when she was interested in something, and while Caleb appreciated her enthusiasm, he knew the plan would not be able to include him.

"So, Jasper has gone and gotten himself hitched." Don smoothly switched topics. Maybe even he could sense Caleb's tension.

"He did," Caleb answered. "I'm happy for him, too. Phyllis seems like a fine woman, and we'll be sorry to lose her at the Morning Glory."

"You still have the best one left," Don winked at Laura before taking a drink.

Had the world tilted? Suddenly, Laura was larger than life, more than his cook, more than his girlfriend. What Don wanted, Don got, and it appeared he wanted Laura as a business partner...and maybe more? How could Caleb criticize the situation? Don was a good guy, a good partner who had helped Caleb expand to where he was now. And Laura, well, he wanted her as a partner, too.

How could a man not?

It was jealousy, Caleb realized, swirling the iced tea in his glass. Even though Laura had invited him to participate, Caleb was jealous. Even though he no longer wanted to be indebted to Don, the green-eyed monster popped up. It wasn't as though he was competing with Don for Laura...or was he?

"What did the hotel offer you for tonight?" Don asked. "Surely, your room won't be dried out. I know my hotel is full because of the conference."

"They offered to find me another room at a different hotel. The dry rooms are all filled for tonight. I was thinking a lot of people would have gone, with the limited presentations tomorrow, but I guess not."

"You could bunk with me, Caleb," Don said. "The suite I've got has a pull-out."

Laura's face showed no outward reaction, but her hand spoke volumes. Slowly, she moved her fingers closer to his groin, inviting him to stay with her another night.

"I think I'm okay, Don. But thanks." He raised his glass to his lips with one hand and moved her hand back down toward his knee with the other. His body was reacting in a predictable, uncomfortable way to her touch.

"I'm glad you decided to stay with me again tonight." Laura grabbed Caleb's hand as they watched Don drive away in his high-dollar Mercedes.

"You kind of convinced me, you little tease." He placed a quick kiss on her lips.

"Don't you like me touching you?" She tried to pout but then laughed, knowing she wasn't any good at it.

"I'm afraid I like it too much, honey. I lose my head when I'm around you."

Hand-in-hand they walked to the elevator and down the hallway to her—*their*—room. The doors on the west side of the hotel stood open, with fans blowing inside, and the windows open so air would flow through to dry off the residue from the sprinkler attack.

She handed him the plastic room key card and followed him inside, clicking on the light. "The message light is blinking." She pointed to the phone next to the large bed.

"Better check it out," he said, heading to the bathroom.

The front desk clerk told her the message was from Mary Grace, saying Caleb needed to call home as soon as possible.

Don't let it be Connor.

As soon as he finished in the bathroom, Caleb called home and got a hold of his brother.

"It's Hank," Caleb told Laura, who was sitting next to him on the bed as he spoke to Josh.

"We're leaving first thing in the morning," He spoke into the receiver. "That'll get us back to the ranch by mid-afternoon. Tell Mom I'm real sorry."

Caleb hung up the phone and hung his head low. "Damn."

"What is it? Is Hank okay?" She placed her hand on the middle of his back to comfort him. "Caleb, is he all right?"

"He was arrested again." He rubbed a hand over his face.

"Again? Good heavens, for what?"

"Drugs." Caleb didn't elaborate.

"Oh." Laura groaned, uncertain what to say. She thought Hank had been hurt or was sick, not incarcerated for doing something illegal. "Connor's okay?"

"He's fine. Holly went out to the ranch to watch him so Mom could bail Hank out."

"Is your mom all right?"

Caleb turned to her and guided her onto his lap, so she was straddling his hips, facing him. She leaned back so she could see him.

"How about we concentrate on something more pleasant?"

Cradling her face, he brought her lips to his. His tongue was insistent, pressing her lips open and tangling with hers. His fingers ran through her hair, urging her even closer. She could feel his need where their bodies met, and she knew what he wanted from her.

Needing a breath, she pulled away. "That was nice." She slid off his lap.

"Where are you going?" He grabbed her hand.

"I'm not sure I'm ready for this." She concentrated on slipping off her shoes.

"We don't have to do anything you don't want to." He sat forward to take off his polished boots. He set them next to the bed and then lay back down on the bed, just as he had the night before, and flipped on the television.

Uncertain, she watched him watch TV. What was she waiting for? Some sign that it was time to move on to the next level with him? She wanted him. Obviously, judging by the bulge in his pants, he wanted her. He admitted to caring about her, asked her to be his girlfriend. What was the problem with her? He wasn't going to propose to her like Jasper had to Phyllis. She didn't want that yet, either. Maybe not at all.

Decision made and with deliberate, cat-like movements, she climbed onto the bed and slowly covered him with her body. "I want you, Caleb," she whispered when her lips reached his ear and then trailed down the side of his neck. She straddled him, liking the feel of his taut body between her legs.

The television went off, the remote hitting the floor with a thud. Caleb's hand found the buttons of her blouse, and he slowly opened the first three, his lips teasing her neck and ear lobe. He pulled her shirt free of her trousers, moving slowly, deliberately as she had minutes earlier. His eyes fixed on hers, almost hypnotizing her with the need she saw there.

She followed his lead, wanting, needing to feel his curly chest hair against her bare breasts. She slipped her shirt off her shoulders and smiled as Caleb's eyes widened. He reached around her back and after two slight fumbles, unsnapped her bra, freeing her breasts for his hands.

"You are glorious." His mouth found each nipple, tasting them with his tongue.

"Oh, Caleb."

She sighed, slightly arching to give him better access before bringing his mouth up to meet hers. She forced him back against the pillows, leaning on him, feeling his strong, muscular chest against her. She fought to free him from the collared shirt he was wearing, and when she succeeded, he pinned her on the bed.

"You like to be on top, do you?" he asked.

She'd indulged in this activity so few times, she'd never been on top. "You take the lead."

He licked and sucked areas on her body she didn't know existed, his hands massaging her shoulders, tummy, and back. When his hands found the button of her pants, she tensed.

"I won't rush things." He spoke breathlessly, his eyes dark with passion. "You tell me when you want to stop, and I will."

"I'm not a virgin, Caleb."

"So you told me." He slowly unzipped her pants. "I'll still stop if you say so."

She lifted her hips, and she moved out of her dress pants, glad she'd purchased the fancy thong panties at the lingerie store. He caressed her outer thighs and then brought his attention back to her breasts, rubbing her hardened nipples with his thumbs, making her wiggle with throbbing desire.

The buckle of his pants gave her trouble, but once it was unlatched, the button and fly opened easily, and he helped her push himself free of the khakis. He was a boxer man. He caught her chuckle in his mouth as he kissed her, guiding her hand to his bottom.

She ached to rip the drawers from his body, rub and caress his manhood, but she waited. If he were even close to as on fire as she was, that would be dangerous. He allowed her to take some of his weight, and instinctively, she wrapped her legs around him, rubbing the back of her calves against the back of his thighs.

"Laura." He moaned and pushed his hardness against her. He found the thin straps that held her thong to her hips and pushed them down to her thighs, opening up her whole world to him. He threw the thong on the floor and slid his tongue along the inside of her thighs. She pulled his head up to hers, not wanting to lose herself just yet.

When the time felt right, she found herself slipping his boxers off his body, him helping her as they reached his ankles. He lay back on the bed on his side and pulled her against him, encouraging her to stroke him. She felt shy, suddenly, not having much experience in pleasuring a man.

"You have a beautiful body, Caleb," she whispered, touching his length, knowing she'd never seen a man built like he was, much less had the chance to fondle one.

He took the hand she was touching him with and kissed it before he let go of her. He stood up and walked to the bathroom counter, where she watched him fumble through his toiletry bag. She watched in awe as the muscles worked in his back and thighs. His size was intimidating, but she knew he would bring her more pleasure than she'd ever experienced.

He smiled and climbed back onto the bed, carrying a foil wrapper, which he handed to her.

"Do the honors?" He kneeled on the bed in front of her, naked and not even the least uncomfortable. Or so it seemed.

She'd never placed protection on a man before, was happy he had something to use. She ripped the foil opened and pulled the sheath out. Going up on her knees, she touched him and slowly slid the prophylactic down his shaft. For a moment, they kneeled in front of each other, neither moving to finish the deed. He kissed her neck and then found her lips. They shared sweet, gentle kisses that made her blood warm.

She lay back and took his hand, pulling him on top of her. She spread her legs and welcomed him to guide himself to her opening. He pulled back slightly, and she closed her eyes, holding her breath, anticipating what she knew would be an amazing sense of fullness.

"I'm sorry, Laura."

Her eyes flew open, and she sat up on her bent elbows, taking in his flushed face.

"I've got a bit of a quick trigger."

The mishap was not discussed that night. They fell asleep holding each other, but he didn't attempt to make love to her again, leaving her wondering what it would be like if he ever did. Laura guessed it was an over-abundance of pride that kept him silent. Really, what could be said that wouldn't embarrass them both?

Jasper and Phyllis were waiting for them at the Casper airport, both smiling as if their lives depended upon it. They'd left Vegas on a red-eye, arriving in Casper on the first flight from Salt Lake City that morning. Jasper looked years younger, with a lighter spring in his step.

The women shared the back seat, and Laura listened quietly to the excited recount of their hasty excursion, her mind fixated on the man in dark shades behind the wheel. What was he thinking? Was he so embarrassed he'd never give it another shot?

"Are you warm?" Phyllis touched Laura's arm in concern.

"Not particularly. Why?"

"You're all flushed in the face."

Laura caught Caleb's small grin in the rearview mirror. Could he know she was remembering how it felt to be touched by him the night before? How his body had caressed her? Maybe he was thinking about it, too. What would have happened if....

It was early evening when they dropped the newlyweds at Jasper's ranch. They'd be out to Caleb's the next day to pick up what was left of Phyllis' stuff. They were excited, Phyllis confided, to start their new life together. Amazing to Laura how much life had changed in just three days.

Laura turned to Caleb as they drove down the long gravel driveway that led from Jasper's house.

"You must be excited to see Conner."

"I hate to be away from him for even this short a time." His expression was hidden in the darkness of the cab. "It was, however, the best conference I've been to in a while. Certainly not boring like a few from the past."

She wondered, of course, if that was due in part to her attendance, but she left the question drop without being asked. In fact, nothing else was said the rest of the trip to the Morning Glory ranch.

Connor shot out of the house the minute Caleb parked the car. He chuckled and climbed down to meet his happy son. A beleaguered-looking Holly followed slowly behind, waving to Laura and Caleb.

"I am so happy to have you home," she said to Laura. "What a mess Hank's in. I feel so sorry for Mary Grace."

Laura had lots of questions but wanted to wait for the time Caleb was ready to share the information with her. It really wasn't any of her business.

She might be involved with Caleb—or after last night, she might not be—but either way, it was his prerogative when or whether to fill in the blanks.

She reached into the bed of the pickup and brought down her suitcase. Laura leaned low to hug Connor when he ran to her side of the truck. She'd miss the little guy, his curiosity, him following her around like her little shadow.

She glanced at Caleb, who was fiddling with something in the cab of the truck, before she walked back to the house with Holly who told her she'd been forced to cook three meals for the men, and in her opinion, Laura was a true miracle worker. Laura swallowed, knowing what Holly said was true, that it would be quite a feat to do it day after day.

The suitcase was heavy, but she hefted it up the stairs and quickly collected the clothing she needed to wash and threw it inside a pillowcase. "Back to real life," Laura said to herself, wondering if the time in Casper had been just a dream.

CHAPTER
FIFTEEN

IN THE DAYS TO COME, she would wonder that over and over again. Had she lived through a dream? Caleb became distant and seemed to intentionally avoid her, spending most of his time away from the house.

The work was pleasing to Laura. She was trying new recipes. It had been so long since she'd cooked anything other than Italian, she branched out to stews and casseroles, much to the delight of the men. The house was sparkling clean too.

Early Friday morning, Caleb and Josh had gone duck hunting at some cabin further in the middle of nowhere than where they lived. He'd kissed her goodbye, even in front of Josh, who took it upon himself to embarrass them with a whistle. And, when he came back late Saturday night, beaming, with eight dressed ducks ready for Laura to cook, he kissed her again, before leaving to spend time with Connor. Of course, she wasn't jealous of his son, but she did miss his company. It was like living in gloomy darkness after having felt the sun on your face.

Sunday rolled around, and Laura was just walking downstairs as the front door slammed open. An older man, clad in overalls and a flannel shirt, burst inside shouting for Mary Grace.

"Where the hell is she?" The man stomped into the kitchen.

"She's not here, Hank," Caleb answered in a calm voice. He stood between Connor and his stepdad. Caleb's calm demeanor settled Laura's nerves enough for her to finish descending the staircase.

From her position just outside the kitchen, Laura could see the kitchen table. A young woman was sitting there, watching the interaction between the two men.

"Where the hell would she have gone, boy? She's got nobody but you and Josh, and I've been there already."

"Jenny, would you take Connor to go find Laura?"

So *that* was Jenny. Laura was filled with anger. What the hell was *she* doing at the ranch at eight o'clock on a Sunday morning? Maybe that was who he'd spent time with last night. Had he lied about being with Connor?

"When did you last see her?"

Caleb continued speaking to his stepdad as Laura met Jenny and Connor in the main room.

Jenny, a very pretty, very *young* woman with blonde hair and light eyes, pushed Connor toward Laura.

"Here she is, squirt," Jenny told Connor. "You probably heard what's going on in there." Jenny turned to Laura. "Hank's off the deep end again. Better stay out of his way. I'm Jenny, by the way." Jenny looked Laura up and down.

"Nice to meet you."

Jenny choked out a laugh. "I doubt that." She laughed again and then wagged her fingers before she left the room and went out the front door.

Laura set aside her jealousy and instead smiled at the sweet little boy standing quietly next to her. She took his small hand and guided him to the back of the house, toward his room. "Let's play with that neat combine I found for you."

She was worried about Caleb and Hank's argument but tried to hide it from the little boy. Just in case, she locked the door to Connor's room, before sitting on the floor and playing farm with him.

The little boy didn't need to be witness to such things.

"I just got out, boy. Your mother refused to post bail, refused to even come see me at the jail. Who the hell does she think she is?" Hank threw Laura's cookbook through the air and it hit the wall.

Caleb swallowed, making himself remain calm. His mother had made poor choices in men over the years. Hank was at least the fifth loser she had been involved with. "Hank, she's not here. You need to leave my house."

"Like you could make me," Hank scoffed. "You're just a wimpy mama's boy."

"Enough! Leave or I will throw you out." Caleb's temper was rising to the bait, despite the energy he put toward trying to remain calm.

"Well tell that bitch mama of yours her days are numbered. When I find her, I'm gonna—"

"You're going to what?" Josh stood in the doorway, fisted hands on his hips.

"You just tell her she needs to watch her step."

Hank pushed by Josh and out the door, climbed in an old jalopy, and peeled out of the driveway.

"Was that Jenny I saw leaving?" Josh asked quietly, coming in and pouring himself a cup of coffee, his demeanor now cool as a cucumber.

"She drove Mom out here last night. Mom got word he was going to be let out this morning. That he finally found someone to bail his sorry ass out." Caleb shook his head.

"Where is she?"

"She's upstairs, hiding. Jasper said he'd come take her out to his ranch if she wanted. I think we need to get a restraining order, don't you? Hank didn't seem to be joking."

"Dealing meth outside the senior high. What a damn fool. I can't believe they let him out."

"They confiscated all the drug crap out of his big building. Just damn lucky Mom didn't get herself arrested, too."

"I messed up again, did I?" Mom, her face tear-streaked, joined them in the kitchen. She looked out the window over the sink and then pulled out a mug and filled it up with coffee.

"We're worried about you, Mom," Josh said. "He's threatening you."

"I guess you can see why I refused to bail him out. I want to wash my hands of the fool. He's facing prison time, and the last thing I want is to be involved with him." She sat at the table and looked around. "Where is Laura?"

"Don't change the subject," Caleb ground out. "We have to contact the sheriff. You need a restraining order. It's the only way to keep you safe."

"You really think a piece of paper will matter to Hank?" Mom laughed without humor.

"Maybe not." Caleb sipped on his coffee. "But anything illegal he does will get tacked onto his prison sentence. He's facing pretty stiff felony charges."

"Fine. Call Brian." Mom's voice was heavy with defeat.

"Mom, would you tell Laura the coast is clear? She's with Connor. I think she's probably in his room." Caleb reached for the phone and dialed Brian.

Maybe Hank was responsible for all the oddities at the ranch over the past few months?

Mom glanced out the window again as she walked to the back of the house.

"I think you were right," Josh said once Mom had left. "Laura is doing a better job than Stella did."

"She is." Caleb listened to the ring of the phone in his ear. He stared at his brother. "Course, I am a bit biased. I'm pretty sure I'm in love."

Laura stopped short at the comment, as Connor and Mary Grace continued into the room. Who was Caleb talking to? And who was he talking about? She caught up to Connor and smiled a greeting to Josh.

"Okay, Brian, we'll see you in a bit. No communication he might hear over his scanner, okay? The man sits beside it like it's a television."

Caleb was on the phone, talking with who Laura could only assume was the sheriff who patrolled through the county.

Caleb ended the call and gave Laura smile. "Good morning. Lots of commotion today."

"Several visitors." Laura reached into the refrigerator and pulled out the orange juice she had put in the pitcher the night before. Pouring some in a glass, she leaned against the counter, studying the Kirkpatrick family.

"I'm just so damn happy to be out here. Last night I was scared out of my wits." Mary Grace shuddered.

"You're welcome as long as need be." Caleb poured milk over Connor's cereal.

"Who wants breakfast?" Laura pulled out her pans. She'd planned an egg casserole for brunch and decided to start a bit early. "Anyone see my cookbook?"

Caleb picked it up from the floor, where it had landed after Hank threw it at him. "Can I help?" he offered quietly, handing her the binder.

"Nope. Thanks."

The image of him and Jenny engaged in the activity that Laura and Caleb had shared at the hotel ran through her mind, and she looked away from him. What could she say?

"I'm headed back home, just wanted to be sure there wouldn't be a problem." Josh kissed his mom's cheek before he left the kitchen.

Caleb stayed where he was, leaning against the stove. Laura stared at him, not able to cook with him there. He crossed his arms and smirked. What did he want?

Mary Grace must have sensed something because she took Connor out of the room.

"I've missed you." He leaned forward into her face as he said it and then leaned back.

"I haven't been the one disappearing," she sniped.

"True, you've been right here all along." He drew her into his arms and gave her a kiss that made her question her anger and jealousy.

"Did you spend the night with Jenny?" she asked as he pulled away.

"No."

"Why was she here? Did you get back from hunting and call her up?" She held her temper but knew she sounded like a jealous hag. "You knew I couldn't satisfy you, so you—"

He cut off her diatribe with his lips. Hands on her rear end, he pulled her against him. She could feel his quick and insistent arousal against her. He parted her lips and tickled her tongue with his, caressing her bottom and the sensitive area of her lower back.

"Trust is hard to come by for you, isn't it?"

"Consider what I've lived through, Caleb. Living with a father involved with the mob, having to go into hiding myself? Yeah, I would say there's a little cynicism in my life right now. A little uncertainty."

"Sorry if I'm adding to the uncertainty." He caressed her cheek. "Not my intent at all. I thought you knew where we stood, Laura. You're my woman." He changed his voice to a silly sing-song at the very end, trying, she imagined, to get a laugh out of her.

"Well, you've got an odd way of being a boyfriend."

"How's that?"

"We haven't spent any time together since we got back from Casper." She hated herself at the moment. She sounded just like a hen pecking at her rooster. "My God, I sound just like my mother." She laughed. Nervous, she went to the fridge and started removing what she needed for her brunch. "I'm sorry. I just, well, I don't know what I expected. It's been so long since I've been with anyone, and we've got an odd circumstance here that we live together, and I work for you, and…."

He came up behind her, and when she turned, he put a finger across her lips to stop her talking.

"How about a date tonight? We'll put Connor to bed early and snuggle on the couch? Watch Netflix or order in a movie? Microwave popcorn?"

"Sounds like heaven," she whispered with a sigh. She stood on her tiptoes and placed a gentle kiss on his lips before he walked to the back door.

"Oh, Laura?" he called.

She returned from the eggs she was cracking in the bowl.

"Jenny drove Mom out here last night. She slept up in the room Angel was in. I imagine she didn't bother to make the bed, so you can go see for yourself."

"Thanks, Caleb."

He walked through the door and poked his head back through.

"I slept in my own bed, just for the record. You're the only woman I'll be touching, Laura, and I expect the same consideration from you."

He'd selected a comedy. She had hoped for a romance to put him in the mood. She popped two bags of popcorn, not willing to share her bag of extra buttered. Connor had cooperated better than they'd expected, going to bed almost as soon as the sun went down.

Caleb had spent the day riding horses with Connor, and when the little boy came inside, Laura had a new coloring book and colored pencils ready for him. She'd watched him while she baked apple pies for dessert and prepared the fresh duck for dinner. She hadn't made duck since culinary school and thought rather than mess it up, she had better refer to the Cooking Channel on the Internet for a recipe.

Now, hours later, Caleb tickled her ear with his warm breath. Chills raced down her spine as he softly kissed the hollow behind her earlobe. She turned her head slightly and caught his lips with hers. Her body tingled on every inch he touched.

The hem of her pullover shirt slid up as his fingers teased the sensitive skin of her stomach, slowly creeping up to cup her breasts.

"Planning this, were you?" he whispered on a chuckle.

"Call it wishful thinking." She'd left off her bra when she'd changed.

"I call it wonderful."

Teasing and touching every inch of her skin, he kissed her as if she was his salvation. Her hands were making a tour of his taut, muscular body. He stoked desire in her veins unlike she'd ever experienced before. This was fun, and she was going to take advantage of every enjoyable moment.

With the buttons of his shirt open, she sat forward to touch her tongue to his nipple. A shudder rippled through his body as he pulled her face back up to meet his mouth.

"Let's take this into my bed."

She nodded, dazed, and held his hand as he led her to his room. He shut the door with a quiet click. He pulled his shirt off and grabbed the hem of hers, ripping it over her head. Her hands found the button of his jeans and slid the zipper down, moving the denim over his narrow hips, down his thighs, to pool at his ankles.

She gripped his bottom and pulled him against her, aching to feel his chest hair tickle her nipples. He backed her onto the bed, and soon she lay before him, naked and willing to share herself. There were no doubts, no second-guessing this time. She wanted him inside her.

He left her, and she could hear a drawer open and close in the bathroom.

He came back to her naked, except for the sheath covering his shaft. "Are you ready, baby?"

"Oh, yes, Caleb, please." She wriggled, feeling as if she would burst if she didn't get satisfied.

He pulled the sheets back and moved her underneath with tender care. Poised above her, he spread her legs, rubbing his finger along the inside of her thighs. His thumb found its way inside her, and she arched. His shaft followed, shooting sparks of delight and satisfaction through her body.

They moved together, rocking in an ancient ritual of pleasure. She reached exquisite fulfillment first, moaning his name so loudly he covered her mouth with his. His breath increased in intensity just as his muscles tensed, and he buried the cry of her name in the pillow next to her head.

He collapsed on top of her, catching his weight with his arms, still kissing her, holding her.

"Thank you," she whispered.

"Oh, no. That was all my pleasure."

"At least you know he works."

"He?" she asked him with a smile.

He chuckled. "My body functions as it should." He kissed the side of her head, loving her scent, her feel. "I never lost it like I did with you at the hotel.

I think it'd just been so long and I wanted you so badly, have fantasized about it since I met you, that when given the chance…"

She pinched his shoulder. "You don't have to explain."

What a relief. He pulled her closer in the circle of his arms.

"Besides," she continued, "you more than made up for it tonight."

"I didn't get to see the end of the movie," he joked, pulling her on top of him, kissing her pretty lips.

She straddled him, and he was amazed to feel his body responding to her again.

"Hold on, tigress woman." He held her hips still. "I don't have any more protection, and while I'm not worried about any weird diseases, I don't think you're ready to give me a baby."

"Can't we just play?" Her mouth trailed the length of him until her lips rested just above his waist.

"Oh, yeah." He sighed. "You go ahead and play all you want."

There wasn't any talking for a very long time.

Sleep came quickly to her, after the full body massage Caleb had given her. Her gentle snores made him smile; it was comfortable holding her in his arms.

As he brushed his fingers through her silky hair, Caleb recalled the question Josh had asked while they were hunting. It was a simple, straightforward question, one only a brother could get away with asking.

"Why didn't you ever marry Christie?"

Josh had just shot his third duck of the day, and they were watching his chocolate Labrador puppy trot off to retrieve it.

It hadn't taken Caleb very long to answer. But he chose to answer with a question. "Why did you marry Holly?"

"Hell, just look at her, Caleb. She might be your sister-in-law, but you can see she's the prettiest thing that would ever be attracted to a mug like mine."

"You married her for her looks?" Caleb knew there was more to it.

"No." Josh bent to pet his dog for a good retrieve. He'd rested the shotgun against his shoulder. "I found her because of her looks, and that's why I dated her off the bat. But I *married* her because she made me feel like a millionaire every time she looked at me, smiled at me." He'd put the duck in the back of his hunting vest and gave the dog a treat. "The first time we had sex, I thought the earth exploded. You know how I was with women. Anything with legs was okay, but with Holly…well…I knew I could never feel anything more with anyone else than what I felt with her. She was it, and I am just damn lucky she felt the same about me."

"I didn't marry Christie because I didn't love her," Caleb had told him. "I cared about her because she gave birth to my son."

"How did that happen, by the way?" Josh asked, pushing his luck.

"What the hell do you mean, how did it happen? You just knocked up your wife, so you obviously understand the birds and the bees," Caleb had said. He chuckled now as he had then. He knew what Josh had meant, and he didn't have an answer.

"Yeah, but we've been trying for two years to get pregnant. We haven't used anything to prevent it. Didn't you and Christie use anything?"

She'd been on the pill. Or so she'd told him. He later found out she'd lied. Connor was proof, but Caleb didn't regret for a single minute the little boy that he'd been blessed with. She left when she recovered from having the baby and never looked back. Caleb didn't miss her, and although Connor probably was lacking in some areas without a mother's love, Caleb had been a pretty damn good dad.

Caleb look down at the woman sleeping so peacefully and thought about his mother. How she slipped into his mind at a time like this, he didn't know, except that maybe he needed to consider her life mistakes as an example. Caleb knew Laura wasn't a mistake, even with a past she was running from and people who wanted her dead.

CHAPTER
SIXTEEN

"I'LL BE OUT AT THE barn all day. Bud called yesterday. He wants pedigrees emailed to him today." Caleb had Laura pinned against the sink in the kitchen, kissing her neck. "Maybe we'll take a ride up there in a week or so and look over his bulls." He turned her and continued kissing the side of her neck in the spot he'd learned over the past few days drove her wild.

She moved slightly, giving him better access. "Your mom offered to take care of Connor and dinner for me. I have sandwich trays ready for lunch, so I'm headed to town to do a little shopping if that works for you."

He pulled back and smiled. "Knock yourself out. Just bring something back for me, okay?" His thumb teased her nipple, visibly taut under the thin T-shirt she wore. "Maybe something you'll save just for my eyes," he suggested with a wink.

He kissed her mouth, started to part her lips but pulled away instead at the sound of a discrete cough from his mother. Laura laughed at his flushed face and moved back to the sink.

"Busted," she whispered.

"Remember what I talked about when you first got here, Laura?" Mary Grace asked her.

"What was that?" They'd had so many bizarre conversations, Laura wasn't sure which one she was referring to.

"The fact that Caleb was a cranky man. And I figured it was because he wasn't getting sex."

"Ma, you didn't." Caleb groaned.

"'Fraid I did," Mary Grace admitted. "I think that's why she's letting you kiss her, Caleb; she's taking pity on you."

"Is that it, Laura?" He pretended to be offended. "Do you feel sorry for me?"

"Yeah, right," Laura said lightly. Then she whispered in his ear, "Think about last night, and then you tell me." She winked before she left the room.

"She's a hell of a good woman," Mom told Caleb after Laura was out of earshot.

"Yeah," Caleb agreed, still looking after her. "You were kidding, right?"

"About what?"

"The pity?"

"Are you blind? The girl's in love with you. Can't you see it? Christ, she's mooning over you."

That made him smile. "You think?"

"I know." Mom placed a hand on his shoulder. "You should marry her, though. All this fooling around isn't good to do in front of Conner. Or God. Plus, you'll never find a better mommy for him, cook for your men, or a wife. She's a hell of a good woman."

"You said that already." He swallowed a gulp of coffee.

"Yes, I did, and I will keep saying it until you admit it."

He watched her leave and knew she was right.

He finished his mug of coffee and left the house, the screen door slamming behind him. Laura had borrowed one of the ranch pickups and was bumping down the gravel driveway as he climbed into his truck. What was he going to do?

Josh liked her. Mom liked her. He and Conner both loved her. She'd made herself part of the family already. It was just a formality to put a ring on her finger—provided she'd agree to wear one.

Was she willing to stay out here? He guessed the only way to find out was to ask her. Mom was an astute woman. And it occurred to Caleb that Jasper was much smarter than Caleb had ever thought.

"What I am saying, Maria, is that I am in love." Laura finally broke down and used the cellphone. She'd left it turned off until the trip into town, paranoid Ernesto would somehow trace it.

"Well, good for you," Maria responded groggily. "But did you really have to call me at six in the morning to tell me?"

"When else was I certain to get you at home?" Laura reasoned as she pulled into a parking spot in Mullen. She had an appointment all the way in North Platte today but was stopping to drop off the ranch's electricity bills and cash her paycheck. "'Sides, it's nine here already."

"So." Maria swallowed a gulp of something. "Have you slept with him yet?"

"Maria!" Laura scolded. "What kind of question is that?"

"The kind only a sister or best friend can ask. Since I'm both, I think you should tell me. Are you needing to see Father William and confess?" Maria chuckled.

"Yeah, I suppose I should. But I'm not really sorry about it, so how can I ask for forgiveness?" Laura said. "Anyway, are you holding up? No problem with Ernesto?"

"Nope, not a peep. Mama Vita and Vinny haven't checked in yet, either. Well, Vin did email me, I guess. But you should see this joint they hooked me up with. It's smaller than our living room at home, I think. There was a really rank odor too, when I first got here; they told me they found moldy salmon in the fridge, but that's cleared away, thanks to some scented candles."

"Candles." Laura smacked her thigh. "That's what I was forgetting." Romance was high on her list of priorities on this trip to town. "Anything else new?"

"What isn't new?" Maria grumbled. "I can't even remember what my cover is, you know? There's this guy, and, well, I'm certain I've tripped over my story at least once. Maybe he's stupid because he hasn't noticed. Or maybe he's sly and just hasn't said anything."

"Is it headed anywhere?" Laura asked quietly. Maria dated a lot but never let her heart get involved. Maybe with her new persona, she'd let herself loosen up and fall in love?

"Who knows? He's a bush pilot. He flies a small cargo plane all over Alaska. I didn't even know how big this state was till I pulled out a map a couple weeks ago. He's gone a lot of nights, so I almost wonder if he doesn't have a second family somewhere."

"You mean like Sammy the Slimeball?"

"Yeah, Pop's best buddy. Slimeball. Hated that guy."

"How are your students?"

"Fun. A lot of fun. Such a different culture out here. The Inuit are friendly. I like it. It's cold and dark now; we have really short days. Might have to get one of those light boxes to boost my serotonin levels."

"I don't have a clue what you're talking about, but do what you need to do." Laura chuckled. "Well, I have to get going. I'm going to the doctor to get birth control."

Maria sputtered into the phone, sounding as if she was choking on whatever she'd been drinking, and Laura laughed.

"I love you very much," Laura said in all seriousness. "Some nights, I miss you so much that it hurts."

"I feel the same, Bre. This is kind of an interesting adventure for us. About time we did something unexpected. I'll be in touch, but not this early in the morning."

Laura hung up and opened the pickup door right into the gut of Tony, one of the Morning Glory's farmhands.

"Oh, geez." Laura scrambled to help him. "I'm so sorry. Are you okay?"

He stared at her for a minute and then nodded.

"You sure, Tony?"

"Yeah, Laura, I'm fine," he bit off and walked away.

She watched him walk off. Why was he so mad? It had been an accident, after all; it wasn't as if she'd deliberately rammed into him. He climbed into one of the other ranch trucks and pulled away from the curb.

She dismissed the encounter and proceeded to the bank, making a mental note of the items she wanted to buy to create a special night for Caleb.

The clock ticked on, time oblivious to the agony Caleb was feeling. The fire danced joyfully in the fireplace, and a pointless television program echoed in the background. He was highly agitated due to anger and fear.

Minutes of waiting for Laura's arrival home had turned into two hours. He drummed his fingers on the arm of the sofa, wondering what on Earth was taking her so long. The town had only a few stores, certainly not enough to keep her there all day, well into the dark of night. He'd picked up his phone a dozen times to text her, only to put it back down. It was her day to spend alone, and he would not be pesky, no matter how much he wondered what the hell she was doing!

Mom was holed up in the bedroom upstairs, hiding. Hank was still out wandering around town. It crossed his mind more than once that in vengeance,

Hank had grabbed Laura while she stopped to pay bills and had her locked in a basement somewhere.

Headlights reflected on the wall, and Caleb shot up to look through the curtains. Relief flooded his veins when he saw the Morning Glory crest on the side of the pickup reflected off the porch floodlights. He sat back down on the sofa and tried to act casual.

The door opened, and he glanced at her. The smile she had on her face stretched from ear to ear.

"Hey, you!" She shut the door and walked over to him and bent down to kiss him.

He turned his face so she hit his cheek.

"What's that about?" She laughed, putting her bags down.

"Where the hell have you been?"

"Shopping." She motioned to the bag sitting at her feet.

"All day?"

"I told you I would be gone all day. As I recall, you said you'd be gone too." Laura plopped on the couch and grabbed the remote, turning the television off. "It was my day off. What are you upset about?"

"There isn't enough to do in Mullen to keep you all day. Did you meet up with someone?"

"No." She frowned. "Who would I see? Phyllis?"

"Tony saw you," he grumbled.

"Yes, he did. I whacked him in the gut with my car door." She chuckled. "I wasn't paying attention and opened it right into him. I guess he told you that though?"

"That and more."

"Would you just spit it out already? What the hell are you so upset about?" She took his hand, but he dragged it away.

"I didn't hook up with a damn soul in town. I went to Mullen, paid the bills like you asked, cashed my paycheck—"

"Who do you love and miss so much that it hurts?" He cut her off midsentence.

"What?"

"Tony heard you on the phone, saying that to someone. Who is he, Laura? Don't lie to me."

"You don't trust me at all."

She grabbed her bags and started to walk away toward her room. A small yellow garment fell out of the bag, and Caleb went to pick it up. He felt his stomach drop. He recognized it as a baby sleeper.

"You can't be pregnant yet. You haven't missed a cycle. Thinking ahead a bit, are you? Don't think you'll be trapping me, Laura."

She ripped it out of his hands. "You said we were going to see Sarah and Bud in a couple of weeks to look at his livestock."

"Yeah, so what does that have to do with—?"

"Sarah is due to have her baby this week! I thought it would be nice to give her a gift." Her eyes shot sparks at him.

Oh, he was an ass, but he wasn't about to admit he was wrong.

"Where did you go today?" This time he asked without accusation in his voice.

"I was trying to tell you. I went to North Platte today."

"North Platte!" Why the hell had she gone down there? "That's an hour and a half away."

"I didn't want people in Mullen knowing my—well, *our* business."

"What does that mean?" The story was going in circles, with no end in sight.

"I went to see a doctor." She flushed scarlet and wouldn't meet his eyes.

"Are you all right?" Suddenly, his anger turned a concern.

"Yes, I'm fine." She lowered her voice. "I went for a prescription for birth control."

"You did?" That was the last thing he'd expected her to say. He'd heard it all before, though; Christie had been bold about admitting to using it when she wasn't. "Let me see it."

"See what?" The frown on her face reached all the way to her eyes.

He was really messing things up, but somehow, he wasn't able to stop himself.

"The prescription." He held out his hand and waved it. "Or the pills or whatever the guy gave you."

She gawked at him, her jaw hanging wide. She shook her head and reached into her handbag and produced the slip of paper. She handed it to him. "It's for a new form of the pill. It's actually a patch," she said quietly, still flushed in the face. She pulled out a small box and let him see what she meant. "I put one of those patches on the first day of my cycle, which should be in a day or two, and switch it every week. Then I don't wear it at all for a week. The doctor, a woman, by the way, said it works just as well as the pill, but I only have to think about it once a week."

He studied the box and swallowed. He'd misjudged her badly. She was trying to move forward and improve their relationship, not break it up, not cheat on him. He was stupid. So stupid he couldn't help but ask, "Who were you confessing your love to on your cell phone?"

"Here." She reached into her purse, pulled out her phone, and threw it at him. "Hit the damn redial and see who picks up." She snatched the prescription and sample box from his hands and stormed from the room, lugging her bags in her arms.

He stared at the phone, wondering if he should ignore it. But he didn't. He figured out the menu and saw that only one call had even registered on the phone. He hit the redial as she instructed and waited as the phone rang.

On the fourth ring, just as he was about to hang up, a woman answered.

"This is Caleb Kirkpatrick," he said right away. "I'm Laura Marshall's boss. I was just wondering why she was calling you."

"Laura Marshall? Who the hell is…? Oh!" The woman started laughing. "You mean Sabrina?" The woman laughed even harder.

"Yeah, Sabrina." It was obviously someone from Laura's past, just not the man he had expected to answer. "Why did she call this number?"

"As I recall, the main reason was to tell me she was falling in love with you, I guess. Yeah, she said your name was Caleb." She laughed again. "I'm her sister, by the way."

Her sister. She called to tell her sister she was in love with him. And he had thought…. Damn, he was stupid.

CHAPTER SEVENTEEN

"Dang it." Laura dumped her handbag on the kitchen counter in frustration. She looked out the window in every direction, wondering if she missed it somehow.

"What's wrong?" Mary Grace looked up from her crossword puzzle.

"Someone took off with the pickup, and I have to run Connor to school." The weather was dismal, a misty drizzle that did nothing more than cool the air and make the skin wet. And flatten her hair.

"One of the men, the smelly big guy, said Caleb told him to change the oil in it. Mac, I think he said his name was? I forgot Connor has school today.... I guess Caleb did too." Mary Grace stood up with a shrug. "No worries, just take the Caddy." Mary Grace opened the drawer closest to the patio and pulled out a heavy set of keys with a remote opener, a rabbit's foot, and a bauble that read Kiss My Grits. She handed the set to Laura.

"Where is it?" It had to be hidden somewhere. Laura hadn't seen it the whole time Mary Grace had been there.

"It's in the back garage. Caleb thought that would be the safest. The only way you get to it is through the door out that way." She pointed through the dining hall area. "There's no side door to come through."

Laura glanced at her watch and then back out the window again. "Connor," she called. "We gotta going."

The little boy scampered in from the main room with his small backpack. After getting a rain jacket on him and throwing a zip-front hoodie on herself, they said goodbye to Mary Grace, grabbed the car seat from the mud room, and were off. The Caddy was cluttered with all sorts of wrappers and empty food bags. Mary Grace, despite her appearance, was a bit of a slob.

Caleb and Josh, in contrast, were neat and tidy. Josh's home was clean, free of clutter, and Caleb's office was too. Where they learned their fastidiousness, Laura could only guess.

She buckled Connor in his booster seat and then started the car, pulling cautiously out into the drive. She was well accustomed to driving a luxury car. Her parents both had similar models, had always liked the gas-guzzler style. The gravel seemed to absorb some of the rain from the night before, and it was soft, rutted, and the car seemed to want to pull the side of the road.

Laura put in a silly song CD she'd grabbed on her way out the door, hoping to keep Connor occupied on the trip to town. It wasn't that long of a drive, but to a six-year-old boy, it seemed like an eternity. Laura considered offering to homeschool him at least the next year but realized the little boy needed the social interaction with other children.

What was Caleb thinking? He hadn't come in for breakfast or coffee as he usually did. He was probably avoiding her. He'd acted like a jerk the night before. He had to learn to trust her or their relationship would end right there.

That thought, coupled with the whacked-out, normal, monthly hormones racing through her body, brought tears to her eyes. Yesterday, she'd been furious with him; now she was scared and sad, worried she'd finally opened her heart up to a man, only to realize she'd made a mistake, and it wouldn't work out because he didn't trust her. She sniffed away the tears, glad Connor was singing along to the CD music and couldn't sense her turmoil.

The wipers weren't terribly effective on the car. Laura would add those to her list of shopping items in town. The combination of small white gravel caked with wet mud and light drizzle was hard to get wiped off the glass well enough for her to see the road ahead. She knew they were getting close to town, as she finally encountered some traffic. People were different out here. They always waved to you, even if they had no idea who you were. Of course, most people recognized Mary Grace's Cadillac.

A light bump and push forward from the rear jolted her. She glanced in her mirrors and could distinctly make out an older, beat-up pickup.

"It's okay, Connor," she soothed, noticing the fear in his eyes. She turned up the CD player a little higher, needing to cover the blood pounding in her ears.

The pickup backed off, and she relaxed with a sigh. Probably just some drunk guy out for a joyride. It was kind of early in the day for that, Laura realized, but she was hard-pressed to come up with another logical reason. She swerved, and the pick-up followed her movements. He sped up and then slowed down. If he wanted the jolt her to scare her, he'd done a good job.

Relax, Laura, relax. She reached for her purse, needing to dial 911, and then remembered throwing her phone at Caleb the night before. She didn't have it. "Damn," she said under her breath.

She glanced in the mirror again, caught Connor's eye, and smiled. Beyond the window of the car, she saw something that turned her smile into a frown, and she gritted her teeth, hoping against hope Connor's seat was secure. "Hold on, honey."

The pickup rammed them harder this time, and Laura struggled to keep the Caddy on the road. "He must be in a mighty hurry," Laura told Connor with much more calm then she felt. "I'll just let him pass." She swallowed her anxiety.

She put on her turning signal and pulled off onto the soft shoulder, but the pickup didn't pass her as she'd hoped; instead, he roared the engine and pushed her with an enormous crushing force into a ditch. The last thing Laura saw was a red truck coming toward them from town, and a cornstalk poking through the broken glass of the windshield.

"Caleb?" Laura whispered, licking her dry, cracked lips.

"I'm here, sweetheart." Caleb moved his chair next to the bed so she could see him without moving her bandaged head.

"Where is Connor?" she asked as soon as her eyes opened.

"With Josh and Holly." He squeezed her swollen hand slightly, careful of the soft cast securing her broken wrist.

"He's okay?" She closed her eyes, big tears rolling from them.

"Thanks to you." He kissed away the tears at the corner of her eyes and sniffed away his own tears. "He's just fine."

Laura nodded and sighed. "Thank God."

"I love you, Laura." He opened his heart to her, swallowing the lump in his throat. "If I had lost you today, I don't know what I would have done. Especially after how I treated you last night."

"You just need to learn to trust me, Caleb." She met his eyes. "I will never hurt you. Not on purpose anyway." With her good hand, she wiped the tears away from her eyes and closed them on a sigh.

"I mean it, Laura. I love you more than anything in the world. You and Connor are my everything. I've never been so scared my whole life. One of the emergency room nurses called me and told me there'd been an accident, that you and Connor were here." He couldn't talk anymore; the pain in his heart was too great. He took a deep breath and tried again. "I will trust you. I will love you and cherish you. I promise. I just wish I hadn't been such a blockhead last night. Can you forgive me?"

She nodded, still crying.

"Do you need anything?" Caleb leaned over her, giving her a smile when she opened her teary, wet eyes again.

"A kiss," she whispered.

"I can do that." He bent forward.

"I need some water too," she told him after he kissed her. "Really cold water."

"I'll get you some."

He pulled away, but she grabbed a shirt.

"Don't leave me. Just buzz the nurse."

He did as she asked. "Anything hurt?"

"No." She shook her head slightly. "Is Connor hurt at all?"

"Bruises but nothing else. The emergency room doctor did X-rays and tests. Josh and Holly came and picked him up an hour or so ago."

"What time is it?"

"Almost three."

"I've been out that long? No wonder I'm so hungry. I didn't even eat breakfast."

"We'll see what the nurse says you can eat." He sat gently on the edge of the hospital bed.

The nurse came in a few minutes later. "There's a sheriff waiting to speak with you, Miss Marshall, when you're up to talking with him." She shut the call light off. "Did you need something?"

"Cold water. I need a drink and something to settle my stomach. Crackers would even work." Laura shifted on the bed. "Oooo, that hurt." She grabbed her side.

"You've got bruised ribs," the nurse told her. "You need to sit still for a bit, and I'll get you some more pain pills in an hour. I'll get you the water now."

"Nurse?" Laura's weak voice caught the woman as she walked out the door. "I'll talk to the sheriff now. I don't want to keep him waiting."

The nurse nodded and left them.

"What's wrong with me?" Laura asked Caleb.

"You got the bruised ribs most likely when the airbag went off. I'm sure you can tell that they are on your left side. Your wrist might have snapped when you hit the ditch; you were probably holding on to the steering wheel, and obviously, from the cast, your right ankle is broken. They think you were hitting the brake, and your foot jammed. You'll be fine, but it might take a while to be fully healed."

"Only that, huh? What a damn mess!" She closed her eyes again. "Do you know who did it? Who pushed us off the road?"

"Don't you?" He brushed the hair out of her eyes. "I figured you would have seen him."

She shook her head, opened her eyes, and was about to answer when someone knocked at the door. She adjusted the sheet and blanket to cover her chest. A uniformed officer walked into the room.

"Laura, this is Brian Nelson." Caleb introduced her. "We grew up together, raised some hell until he became the sheriff." He patted Brian's back. "You can trust him, Laura."

Brian pulled out a small notebook from his breast pocket and sat on the upholstered chair next to the bed. He was opposite in looks to Caleb, blond with blue eyes, broad shoulders, and narrow at the hip. The sheriff's uniform made him even sexier, but Laura wasn't interested in his looks.

"I'm sure sorry you got hurt, Laura. Why don't you start at the beginning?" he said. "I have an eyewitness who saw the actual accident, but I'd like to hear your take on it."

"Is your witness the man in the red-and-white pickup? He passed us just before we got knocked off the road."

"Yep, that's him," Brian answered.

"Everything was fine until I was just about to town. I didn't even see another vehicle the whole way. Connor and I were singing a song, and suddenly, something jarred the car. I looked in the rearview mirror and saw an old pickup behind us. The back window was pretty dirty, but I could see pretty well out my side mirrors. An old beater. I figured he was just in a hurry to get to town, and then he backed off, and I thought maybe he was drunk. He sped up again, so I pulled over to the side of the road, onto the shoulder, thinking he would just pass us. But he didn't. He hit the car really hard. We flew into the ditch, and that's all I remember."

"Would you be able to identify the truck?" Brian looked up from his legal pad.

"Yes, I am pretty sure I could."

"Did you get a look at the driver?"

Brian glanced at Caleb before looking at her.

"No." She shook her head and then moaned. "All I saw was a cowboy hat. Which just about every man wears out here. This witness you mentioned? Did they get a look at the driver?"

"Yes. They identified someone. I can't say more than that right now. We have that person locked up already in Mullen."

"Was it someone local?"

Caleb knew what she was worried about. The Chicago thugs. He knew also who they had arrested for the accident, but he'd promised Brian he wouldn't tell her.

Brian stared at her for several seconds, his blue eyes pinning her against the pillow. Thank goodness she wasn't in trouble with the law; those eyes were so intense they seemed to look into her very soul.

"Yes, it's someone who lives in Mullen." Brian gave an abrupt nod.

"Why didn't you take the pickup you normally drive?" Caleb didn't understand why she'd had his mother's vehicle, and he had forgotten to ask his mother when he told her about the accident.

"That was my question too. Why did you have Mary Grace's car?" Brian scribbled something down on the paper.

She explained about the pickup's disappearance.

"I never did that." Caleb shook his head, frustrated. "I never told Mac to do any such thing. Ronnie always does the repairs and maintenance on the engines."

"Maybe Mary Grace got it wrong."

"No matter. I didn't tell anyone to do anything with the pickups today or any day in recent memory."

"Anything else you can think of?" Brian asked and stood to leave.

"No." She closed her eyes and leaned back in the bed. "But if I do, I'll let you know."

"It wasn't your fault, Laura." Brian patted the cast on her hand. "You did good. The way that car was hanging...well, that ditch was more of a ravine and, well..." Brian shook his head and glanced warily at Caleb. "Take care of yourself. I'll talk with you again." He left them, closing the door behind him.

"How long do I have to stay here?" She wiggled under the covers to get a comfortable spot.

"Just overnight. I'll stay with you. I already told Josh and—"

"You should be with Connor," Laura interrupted him. "He'll be scared, don't you think?"

"I told you, he had just a few bruises. He loves staying with my brother and Holly. It's you I'm worried about."

"Why?"

"Because I love you, and I would feel better if I was here with you, taking care of you."

Pain shot through her chest, waking her up in the middle of the night. She'd refused her last dose of pain medicine before she went to sleep, and now she was regretting it. She felt around for the nurse's call button and was relieved when she pushed it in and saw the light glow in the darkness of the room.

A new nurse must have come on since Laura had fallen asleep. She told her in whispered tones that she needed her medicine, and that her side felt like there was a nail stuck in it, and both her wrists and ankles were throbbing. She felt miserable and hoped the pills would kick in fast. The nurse took her temperature and other vitals after she gave her the pills.

"All normal?" Laura asked quietly.

"You bet." The nurse looked over to Caleb. "He doesn't look too comfortable."

"No, but I'm glad to have him here," Laura admitted, feeling selfish.

He loved her. He'd admitted it, and if actions spoke louder than words, seeing him in a chair next to the bed, with his long legs propped up, showed dedication. And discomfort.

"If these don't kick in soon enough for you, buzz again. It's a quiet night tonight. Your husband can sleep in the other bed. I don't expect any admissions this late at night."

"I'll tell him if he wakes up."

"I'm awake," Caleb told her as soon as the nurse left.

"Not too comfortable for you."

"I imagine you're no more uncomfortable than I am, honey." He grinned.

"How about you crawl up here with me?" Laura suggested.

"Right. As much pain as you're in? No way? 'Sides, it's probably the drugs talking." He stood and stretched. "Do you want more water?"

"Yes, please." She nodded. "The nurse put it on the side table."

He handed it to her. "Mind if I use your potty?"

She chuckled. "Have at it. I don't need it."

Such intimacy. Except for her family, she'd never felt this comfortable with another person. It was scary really, that he'd climbed his way into her heart so fast.

When he came out, he wheeled the big, empty bed next to hers and sat on the edge to remove his shoes. He threw his legs up on the bed and lay back on the pillows.

He reached out and took her hand and squeezed it. "Feeling better?"

"Sleepy," she said, smiling. "The pills are kicking in quickly, I think."

She closed her eyes, feeling loved and cherished, just as he had vowed he would make her feel.

"MAMA VITA, WHAT THE HELL are you doing here?" Laura woke up to a shocking surprise the third day after her accident.

"I got a call from Vinny." She held up one diamond-ring clad finger. "Who got a call from Maria." She raised another finger. "Who got a call from your boss?" Her hands went to her hips. "I tell you, Sabrina, you ought to tell your mother when things like this happen. I shouldn't be the last to know."

"But it's not safe for you to be here with me." Laura tried to sit up but failed in the effort. Her ribs were still too tender and bruised. She eased back onto the pillows. "When did you get here?" She would only admit it to herself, but she felt better with her mother there.

"An hour ago. I tell you, Sabrina, this place is in the middle of nowhere. Even with the GPS system, it was nearly impossible to find. I can't believe people actually live out here." Mama sat on the bed. "I can't believe you're sleeping in your employer's bed. That's not quite right." She looked around the room then and reached toward the dresser and tentatively touched the mounted, stuffed pheasant sitting there. She made a face. "Isn't this a bit odd?"

"He's a hunter." Laura ignored the censure in her mother's voice and closed her eyes on a sigh. "If you switch on the light, you'll see a deer head over there."

Mama Vita flipped on the light and took a step back. "Oh, my."

Laura laughed and then groaned at the pain in her side. "Ouch, ouch, ouch." She shifted on the bed. "Help me up, Mama Vita. I have to use the bathroom and take some of those miracle drugs."

Her mother helped Laura slip out of bed and gave her the crutch. The cast on her leg was heavy, and she felt clumsy. She took care of her needs and swallowed the horse-sized pills before she wobbled back into the bedroom. Mama Vita was sitting on the edge of the bed, studying her fingernails.

"Tell me that you're all right." Laura took Mama's hand with her good right one.

"I can't stay in Florida; I hate it there." Her hand sliced through the air. "Too hot, no wind. It's sticky. But other than that, yes, I am fine."

Laura bent forward and kissed her forehead.

"I'm fine," Mama said, "but I am here to make sure you are."

"I hurt," Laura said. "I'm bored and tired of being in bed."

"Well, let's get you up and out of here," Mama said. "Where are your clothes?"

"Upstairs, in the end bedroom." She sighed, feeling the room spin out of control, and sat back onto the bed.

"You sit then. I'll find something for you to wear."

Mama Vita left Laura pondering on the bed. In all her years, Laura had never so much as strained a muscle. Even with her daily exercise, or maybe because of her physical exertion, she'd never been injured.

Mary Grace was filling in for Laura, cooking and cleaning, until her ribs were good enough for her to stand straight. The poor woman hadn't stopped crying around Laura since she'd gotten out of the hospital, so Laura had hidden out in Caleb's bedroom. She couldn't climb the stairs with her leg, so he'd swapped with her. At least, she imagined he was sleeping in her bed.

"Hi, Laura." Connor poked his head around the corner. "How are you today?"

"Much better." She opened her arms wide and welcomed the little boy to her. Careful of her ribs, she held him as tightly as she could. "What should we do today? Do you want to color or play Go Fish?"

"Can you?" Conner's eyes were huge.

"Sure." She kissed the top of his head. "My mom came to see me. Do you want to meet her?"

He nodded.

"She'll help me get dressed and then we can play."

"Okay, I'll go get my cards and pencils."

Laura looked up to watch him leave and found Caleb leaning on the doorjamb.

"And you thought he would be mad at you?" He ruffled his son's hair as he left the room.

"I didn't know," she admitted. "I just hoped he would know it wasn't my fault."

"How are you today?" He walked over to her and lifted her in his arms. "I'll be gentle," he whispered before he dropped his lips on her.

A discrete giggle from Mama Vita as she entered the bedroom drew their attention.

"So, that's how it is, huh?" she asked.

"Fraid so," Caleb admitted. "I'll go get the other surprise, Vita, and be right back." He set Laura gently on the bed and left the room.

"Another surprise?"

"This is a good one," Mama Vita said.

A few minutes passed, allowing Laura to pick out some clothes that might fit over her casts and that weren't too tight on her ribs.

"Hello, Princess."

She looked up at the deep voice. "*Pop?*"

In the doorway stood her father. It was as if she was seeing a ghost. "What the—?"

"Hi, baby Bre." He walked into the room and gingerly hugged her.

Tears streamed down her face. "You're not dead." She repeated the phrase over and over, unable to think of anything else to say.

"Had to go undercover. Had to pretend to die."

"Oh, my goodness, I am so happy, I can't even say."

Laura glanced from her father to Caleb, who stood in the doorway grinning.

It felt like her life was complete again, but far fuller than it had been because Caleb and Conner were now a part of it.

"I guess I should fill you in on what we've learned about your accident." Caleb settled her on the porch. It was almost Thanksgiving, a full month after she'd been run off the road, and they were enjoying an unseasonably warm stretch of days with temperatures in the sixties.

"Please?" She took a sip of hot chocolate. It was amazing to Laura how well Mama Vita was handling Connor, how well she was getting along with

Mary Grace. Laura was sitting in an odd position on the screened-in porch, her leg up in the air, her opposite wrist elevated. The sun was just about to set, and she felt well despite not taking any pain pills since early that morning. Maybe movement and activity were the keys to her recovery.

"I've kept the newspaper away from you intentionally." Caleb leaned back in the chair, crossing his ankles and folding his arms against his chest. "I'll show them to you if you want. They had pictures of Mom's car, how it landed cockeyed in the ditch. There's the explanation of the accident too."

"Just as long as my picture isn't in the papers or on television, everything will be fine." She set her mug down. "It's bad enough my parents are here."

"I don't expect a problem with that. We did have a couple of reporters call. I did the best I could when they asked about you without telling them anything about you." Caleb chuckled. "I had a hard time being evasive, but I think I ended up doing fine. I'll let you see the articles."

"How about you tell me who hit us, Caleb?" Laura knew he knew. Figured he'd known already when she was in the hospital. He and Brian were such good friends; the sheriff had surely told Caleb who he had arrested.

"It was Hank." Caleb shifted, looking uncomfortable with the admission. "He thought you were Mom taking Connor to school or coming to town. He admitted his guilt already. There won't need to be a trial—he'll just serve his sentence. No chance of bail this time, either. He'll have these accident charges and then compound them with the other drug charges."

Laura digested the information, her gut turning. At first, when she realized what had happened, she'd worried it had been or Ernesto Garbaldo, that he had found her, hired someone to get rid of her as punishment for what her father had done to him. In the hospital, when Brian told her it was someone local, she had felt relieved. Now knowing it was Hank, her pain changed from a selfish one to more of concern and sadness for Mary Grace and for Caleb and Josh, who would deal with the scandal of their stepfather's stupidity.

"Was he ever a good man?" Laura finally asked in deflated, hushed tones.

"I thought he was okay." Caleb shrugged. "I never lived with him or spent a whole lot of time with him though. I was in my late twenties when he started sniffing around Mom. Josh was still at the house in town, living with her, but really, Josh was out here more than not."

"Is that why Mary Grace cries every time she sees me? She feels responsible?"

"She's embarrassed that she married the guy but also upset that she was supposed to be the one in the car and even worse that the idiot didn't care Connor was in the car." Caleb pulled her against him. "He has such an ugly vendetta, almost an obsession toward her, for refusing to bail him out and then leaving him. I guess he just saw red."

"It's not her fault." Laura suddenly felt as if the weight of the world was on her shoulders. "Caleb, I have to ask, although I will hate myself for doing it." She wanted to put it as delicately as she could. "Did she know what he was up to?"

He stared at her for the longest minute, and she found it difficult to breathe. Had she just made him mad, hurt his feelings?

"I don't think so," he told her quietly. "But I can't say for certain." He lowered his voice even further. "There have been things missing here at the ranch. Things I didn't think much about, but Brian tells me it's all related."

"At least you know there aren't a bunch of people out to get the ranch."

"Stella called yesterday. One of Juan's kidneys had quit, and the other is damaged. He'll need dialysis, and they put him on a transplant list."

"How horrible!" Laura's injuries were minor compared to Juan, a man who was fighting for his life.

"I was wondering." Caleb paused. "Would you be willing to split duties with Stella? She needs the job, and it sounds like they can help Juan with the dialysis right at the hospital in Mullen."

"Of course, I'll do that. I had planned to work with Phyllis anyway."

"Thank you." He caressed her cheek with the back of his fingers. "I wish you were feeling better. I would sure like to roll around with you in bed right now. To comfort you, show you just how much I love you." He sat forward and kissed her with gentle pressure.

"You're welcome to share your bed, Caleb," she told him when he pulled away.

"Where the hell do you think I've been sleeping?" He laughed and pinched her earlobe. "I've been a damn nursemaid, fluffing your pillows and making sure your hand and leg are elevated for the last three nights. Dodging your cast as it about whacks my head off." He laughed again. "You didn't know?"

"No." She shook her head, stunned. "I must have been sleeping pretty soundly to miss feeling you next to me." She leaned into his lips and felt the intense desire brew, just as she always did when they connected. "Thank you." What else does a woman say when she learns the man she loves has been slaving away and losing sleep because of her?

"It's the pills. You're taking an extra one at night for sleeping. They seem to knock you out almost immediately."

She nodded, remembering that but still amazed she could sleep without knowing his body was next to hers.

"I told Mom she could have her choice of the pickups out here, that I'd be buying a different vehicle." He rubbed his thumb over her bottom lip. "What do you think about a minivan? Fill it with a handful of babies?"

"A handful?" That sounded exciting.

"Three, maybe four." He shrugged. "I'm easy. Connor needs a baby sister."

"So you're saying I shouldn't bother with the patch thing?"

"That depends if you're interested in marrying me or not."

She was afraid the pain medication was muddling her mind. Did he just ask her to marry him?

"You said you'd never get married," Laura argued.

"When did I say something that crazy? Certainly not after we made love." He kissed her. "I knew then, well, actually, in Casper before *the incident*, there was no way I'd ever let you go."

He dropped to one knee and took her hand.

"Marry me, Sabrina Marconi. Lose the Marshall name forever and marry me."

He looked scared and serious, like a rabbit just before a car hits it.

"Why?" Laura wanted the words. "Just so we can give Connor siblings?"

"Because I love you more than any man has ever loved a woman," he told her simply. "Because you have brought joy and happiness into my life and to Connor's life in a way we never had it before. Because the thought of living without you in my life, even for a day, is suffocating."

The tears spilled out then, choking her throat.

"What a proposal." She chuckled, wiping away the water from her eyes. "How could I say no?"

CHAPTER
NINETEEN

THEY ARRANGED FOR THE WEDDING to be held at the courthouse just a few days later, as soon as Laura was able to stand in front of the judge. Her parents didn't feel safe sticking in one place too long. They had been touring the country in an RV, stopping at campgrounds along the way, and learning to like the simple life. Mama Vita was even cooking and cleaning.

"Mama Vita!" Laura called out from her place on the couch in the main room of the ranch. "Vinny's on the news. He's been arrested. Aw, hell." She punched the volume on the remote higher to hear the Chicago anchorman elaborate on the crime.

Racketeering.

Laura's parents rushed in from the kitchen, where they had been visiting with Caleb and his mother and joined her on the couch.

Caleb stood behind her and rested his hands on her shoulders. "He certainly looks like you."

The FBI wanted to flip Vinny, to get him to testify against the Garbaldo family. To this point, he'd refused to rat on the mafia boss—doing so could very well implicate himself in illegal activities. Vinny knew far more than Laura or Maria knew about the business end of the Garbaldo family. Their testimonies would help build a case against Garbaldo, but then Vinny could put him away for a very long time. He was Garbaldo's stockbroker, and only he and the Lord knew where some of the Garbaldo money had been stashed and laundered.

"Damn." Bobby Marconi watched his son being led away in handcuffs. "They're bringing him from North Carolina back to Chicago."

"What will he do?" Caleb asked.

Laura turned over her shoulder to look at her new husband, still shocked they were married. His gaze was fixed on the TV.

"Depends what kind of deal they offer him." Laura squeezed the hand still resting on her shoulder.

"That's Garbaldo, huh?" Caleb asked as the bald, fat, late-middle-aged man walked in front of cameras, that signature cigar hanging from his mouth.

"Bastard," Laura's father said. "He ought to be dead."

"What can we do, Pop?"

She felt helpless, didn't know if there was anything anyone can do to help Vinny but Vinny himself. It wasn't as if he was the only one still in danger either. Anyone in the room could be next.

"We better be leaving, Bobby," Mama Vita said. "I don't think it'll be good for us to be around here much longer. We are like sitting ducks out here."

"Quiet, Vita, he's talking."

Sure enough, Ernesto Garbaldo sauntered up to the microphones.

"Let me tells you all something," he started. "Vinny Marconi ain't done nothin' wrong." He pointed his finger holding the cigar at the reporters.

"What about the rest of the Marconi family?" a reporter yelled. "How about Bobby Marconi's daughters? Mrs. Marconi?"

"Vita? I got too much respect for her to be in any further contact. Sabrina ain't got nothing to worry about neither. She took a bullet for her worthless father and made her amends to me another way."

He stepped away from the reporters, flipping them the bird after he shoved his stogy back into his mouth.

"Maria?" Laura squeaked, her stomach knotting itself.

"He didn't mention her, did he?" Bobby stood and started to pace. "That's probably a good thing. At least he thinks I'm dead. Vinny's got a damn hard decision to make. Damn, I wish I could help him."

"Laura, what did he mean that you made amends to him?" Caleb walked around the couch and sat in a nearby chair.

"Let me guess." Mama Vita turned to her. "Bella Vita."

Laura nodded, the lump in her throat holding her back from saying anything.

"You gave him your restaurant, Laura?" Caleb's sad expression surprised Laura. "You gave him everything you had?"

"Not quite," Vita answered for her. "Our Sabrina is about as thrifty as they come. Vinny would spend every penny he got. Laura squirreled it all away."

"I have enough to get by," Laura answered. "I guess now that we're married, it's yours too." She chuckled. "You really won't need an outside investor anymore."

"That much?" The muscles at the sides of Caleb's jaw tensed as he ground his teeth together.

"We'll talk later," Laura said. "Where are you going to go?" she asked her parents, looking from Mama Vita to Pop.

"I want to be in Chicago, but I don't think that would be such a good idea," Mama Vita said.

"He's not out for you though," Laura told her. "Could you go and give Vinny your support and advice?"

"No," Pop said. "She ain't going nowhere near Chicago. Vinny's an adult, he's going to have to dig himself out of this one."

"Alaska?"

"Not now, no," Pop said. "Alaska in November doesn't sound too appealing. Plus, Maria isn't in any danger." He stood. "We only came here because you were hurt."

"Thanks." Laura smiled.

Mama Vita stood. "Let's go, old man."

She bent down and kissed Laura on each cheek and then kissed Caleb too.

"You take good care of her, Caleb," Pop said. "I still have connections." He winked. "Email us when we become grandparents, would you?"

Later in bed that night, in the silence of the western Nebraska Sandhills ranch, husband and wife contemplated their future together.

"So, you're telling me we're rich?" Caleb stroked her back, right where the bullet went through her side.

"Not rich, maybe, but now you've got money to play with, to make the ranch grow sooner rather than later." She rolled on top of him, careful not to kick him with her walking cast or hit him with her wrist cast. "'Course, once my cookbook makes the bestseller list, we might be. And when Morning Glory Organics takes off, the sky's the limit." She chuckled. "I love you." She kissed him on his collarbone, loving the feel of his warm skin beneath her lips.

"Remind me to tell Josh thank you."

"Your naked wife is lying on top of you and you're thinking about your brother?"

He pinned her on her back. "If it weren't for him, I wouldn't have you."

"Wonder if I would have won if Angel hadn't screwed up and if Phyllis hadn't gone off with Jasper to get married?"

"What do you think?" His hands were working their magic, taking away any doubt in her mind.

She was the winner, in more ways than one.

ABOUT THE
AUTHOR

JULIA DANIELS writes happily-ever-after stories with a hint of mystery. A Midwesterner born and bred, she enjoys using the settings of small farming communities to watch love blossom and grow!

Julia lives in Nebraska with the love of her life and their two children. Her author page at Amazon.com can be found here:

www.amazon/Julia-Daniels

OTHER BOOKS BY JULIA DANIELS

Master of Her Heart

The Earl Next Door

Duchess on the Run

Choices of the Heart

FIND JULIA ONLINE

WEBSITE:

www.juliadanielsbooks.com

FACEBOOK:

w www.facebook.com/JuliaDanielsBooks

TWITTER:

@ScribeJulia

BLOG:

www.juliadaniels.wordpress.com

JULIA DANIEL'S READING GROUP:

www.facebook.com/groups/538945183153970

GET BOOK DEALS AND DISCOUNTS

Get discounts and special deals on books at

www.TCKPublishing.com/bookdeals